Public Library
DeKalb, Illinois
RULES

1. Books may be retained for two weeks and
   may be renewed once for the same period
   unless otherwise indicated.
2. A fine is charged for each day that library
   material is overdue.

SWAN'S WING

SWAN'S WING

URSULA SYNGE

THE BODLEY HEAD
LONDON SYDNEY
TORONTO

British Library Cataloguing
in Publication Data
Synge, Ursula
Swan's wing
I. Title
823'.914 (J)   PR6069.Y7S/
ISBN 0-370-30425-X

© Ursula Synge 1981
Printed in Great Britain for
The Bodley Head Ltd
9 Bow Street, London WC2E 7AL
by Redwood Burn Ltd,
Trowbridge & Esher
First published 1981

Part One

Part One

My cathedral grows. The twin towers of the west front already dominate this little town, the nave is roofed at last. Today woodcarvers moved into the choir and the air is sweet with the smell of shavings, their sweetness mingling with the acrid smell of stone dust that is always present. In another twenty years it may be finished and, by then, I will be an old man leaning on a stick, telling the young builders that our ways were best, that in their struggle to be original they have abandoned art. That is the way age takes us all.

Even now, while I am at the zenith of my life, I find myself looking back and sighing for certain days I can never have again, and for certain people— three or four, perhaps—whose company I miss. I say to myself, 'The world is not what it was . . .' and laugh, for men have been saying this since the days of Abraham and before—though it is true, I think, that the only wonders to be found in recent years are those we make for ourselves. Enchantment is confined to fireside tales and if we chance to meet it in our waking lives we say nothing, knowing that such treasure is spoiled by daylight. But mostly we see only what is in front of us—wood and stone, cobwebs and dust and, if we are lucky, the play of light among leaves. Nevertheless, we should be wary—things are not always what they seem.

It was a hard winter. The snow came early and stayed late, lying on the ground till April, and the sky still heavy with it. Many of the old people died that year and were buried with less mourning than was decent. The kine, kept too long in cramped quarters and short of fodder, starved and sickened. It was a bad, hungry year—and it was the year when Hodge the woodman found an abandoned child in Low Spinney and took it home with him. His wife, good woman that she was, bade him take it back.

'And let the foxes eat 'un?'

'Why not?' she said. 'They be as famished as we.'

But that was empty talk. Foundling or no, it was a human soul, the priest said, and they must care for it. So the baby, something less than a year old, was passed about from one poor dwelling to another, warmed a little, fed a little and loved not at all. People said it must be of the Devil's getting for it thrived on the most meagre of scraps and seemed not to mind the cold as mortal babies do.

'A human child would 'a perished in the snow long afore Hodge found thic 'un,' they said. And they gave the spinney a new name—the Devil's Spinney. When the priest heard this he was angry and made a long sermon on the virtues of charity. He said the village was no better than a heathen place that it should harbour such thoughts, but it was easy for him to talk—he had not the rearing of the creature. Yet he did what was better, in his eyes. He made the cross on its head with Holy Water and named it Matthew. A proper baby cries at its name-giving so that the sin in which it was conceived flies out of it to some other place, and wise godparents put salt on the infant's tongue to make certain that it will bellow at the right moment. This must have been neglected in Matthew's case for, when he felt the water on his brow, he chuckled and put out his fist to beat at the priest's hand. Surely that was right proof of the child's paternity, if proof were needed.

The years passed in expectation that sooner or later the Devil would reappear to claim his own but, in this, the village was disappointed. Matthew remained among them. He was small, ill-favoured and without friends; the other boys called him *Devil's get* and threw stones at him. He was not big enough to fight them and not brave enough to stand his ground so he ran away, whenever he could, and hid in a secret place he made for himself near a pool where the moorhens nested. There, he hugged his bruises and wondered how it was that the words hurt harder than the stones, though they left no mark on him that he could see. That way he learned early and thoroughly that a man is something more than his skeleton clothed in flesh and sinew, though perhaps others learn it with fewer pains.

The animals seemed not to mind him as the village people did. He even played with the little foxes while the vixen sat by—and one night he saw a badger family move from its sett, going in single file through the undergrowth quite near where he lay hid, and later he found the place where they had buried the Old One, and, having found it, scraped away the earth to uncover the corpse. He had known about death for a long time but this was the first dead thing he had ever seen closely, the first he had touched and it troubled him. He whispered, 'Dead!' and again, 'Dead!' but the word had no meaning for him beyond the state it described— carrion. It said nothing of where the life of the badger had fled, or what made the difference between life and death. He saw that the badger's eyes were dull and wondered if that was the mystery, if life were seeing and death, not seeing.

Matthew thought about that a little longer. Then he closed his eyes slowly, noticing what he did, and he was still alive. He could move, his limbs were not stiff as the badger's were. After that he went about with his eyes tight shut until he could find his way as well in the dark as by daylight and was certain that life had nothing to do with seeing. In the dark he learned to hear. He learned to distinguish each beast by the sound it made, he thought he could hear the trees growing. And life had nothing to do with hearing. With his eyes closed and his hands over his ears, he could still move and he could still think.

He went back again to where he had left the badger's corpse but crows and foxes had been before him and there was nothing left but a scattering of bones with a swarm of blue flies busy above them. There was nothing to be learned from those.

In the village Mag, the miller's wife, sat with her gossips in the sun. Their tongues were busier than their spindles for Mag was heavy with her first child and every other woman was eager to talk of her own birthing and to give advice. Heads together and voices lowered, they did not see Matthew squatting nearby until, strain- ing to hear what they were saying, he came too close. Mag screamed like a screech owl and covered her face, and all the women rose at once in a scolding group to hide her from the sight of the Devil's bastard. One made the sign of the horns with her outstretched fingers while the rest bustled Mag away to safety.

'I've done nothing,' he said. 'I never touched her.'

'You were listening and watching, you sly toad.'

'I like to watch,' he said. 'Missus Mag's gentle and kindly. I'd not harm her.'

'Not harm her! Don't you know it's a bad time for a woman even to be seeing such a thing as you?'

'I've done nothing,' he repeated. But he could not be sure, and these women were very sure that he had the power to blight, by merely being there, the unborn child in the womb. And they were afraid, therefore it might be true.

For whole long days Matthew sat in his secret place, thinking about these two great mysteries—birth and death—and about all the fears that lay between them. He thought of the badger's sightless eyes and the stiffness of its body.

'Death ends it,' he said. 'After death there be no more running and no more fear. But do it begin with birth?' There was movement before birth, he knew. He had seen Mag's belly move as her child kicked; he had seen her put her hand to the place where it stirred and she had smiled, secretly, as though she and the child spoke together. She had been afraid for its well-being too, afraid it would be hurt by his looking, the way he had been hurt by words. Perhaps the unborn have fears that we can never know.

So he sat, struggling to make sense of it, when suddenly he was roused by a moorhen's shrill *krerrk* of alarm, almost at his feet. While she kept up her agitated *kick-kick-kittick-kick*, he parted the reeds to see what had disturbed her. At first there was only the white dazzle of the sun on the water which made him blink, and then he saw a wild cat, crouched on a low shelf where a part of the bank had fallen away. She was pitifully thin, her shoulders almost pierced the harsh striped fur, and Matthew knew that only extreme need could have driven her to quench her thirst so openly. When she saw the boy's face peering at her from between the reeds, she hissed and made to dart away but one of her hind-legs dragged and would not bear her weight. Matthew had time to see that she was not only lame and starving but also gravid, her sides bulging with new life—and she was brave. He liked that. He watched her go, marking well what path she took.

That night he stole for her—a scrag of mutton, none too fresh, and a pannikin of milk which was awkward to carry, spilling a little as he climbed up through the woods. She had made her bed in a hollow among the roots of a dead tree, a lair deserted by foxes. Matthew set down the food and waited. The smell of meat soon drew her out and, though she saw him, she was too far gone in misery either to attack or to run away. She made a little yattering noise with her mouth, the way a farmyard tabby does when it watches birds, and then took the meat in one bite, snarling over it and jerking her head so that saliva spattered the ground like drops of rain. Still watching Matthew, she drank. Her eyes were two fierce moons in the dark. She would not accept him as a friend and that made him glad, he wanted no friendship he could buy with food.

Her hunger sated, she sat upright, forepaws neatly together, her head very small and fine above the swollen shape of her body. Her manners were fine too. Memories from a better-ordered life stirred within her skull. She licked a paw and very carefully washed her face and muzzle. Then she froze, her mouth protesting as a shiver ran through her fur and then another so strong that she almost fell. She whimpered and dragged herself to the furthest corner of the lair and Matthew followed, as near to her as he dared. She showed her sharp teeth, resenting his presence, but there was no time now for anything except what was demanded of her.

Matthew held his breath, afraid that she would die. But cats do not die so easily and this one knew what she was about. She twisted round and began to lick her belly with long slow strokes of her rough tongue—down and down again and down—but it was an age before the first kitten came, damp and mewling, into its separate life. The mother sniffed it, kicked it into the comfort of her side and went again to the work. Four kittens she licked from her vent while Matthew stayed with her, and it seemed to him that he too was born that night. He knew now what it meant to be *born*, and how life begins. It was better, richer and more terrible to be born than just to be found, alive, in a wintry wood—but he did not think at all of his own mother who had birthed him, kept him with her for a while, and left him there.

He visited the cat every day. When he was unable to steal for her he took his sling and shot birds or tickled for fish in the stream. These were gifts of love and gratefulness and she accepted them and grew sleek. The kittens clambered all over her and over each other, squealing and burrowing into her fur. Their bellies were round, their blind heads blunt and thrusting, their tails held erect like little spears.

The kittens opened their eyes, a piercing blue which soon changed to the same dark gold as their mother's—and Matthew's eyes opened too. He found a world worth seeing and one he wanted to keep.

One day he took a reed and scratched lines in the dry earth—a long curve for the she-cat's back, four fat ovals for the young ones. This was something new and he was pleased at first but later, seeing the faults in it, he was ashamed and scuffed it away with his heel. Yet it was a beginning. His next attempt was better, the next better still.

That was the cat's gift to Matthew. She taught him to look for the pattern in what he saw, to think of movement as the change from one shape to another. And his hands learned from his eyes. Everywhere he went in the woods he left pictures, sketched on earth and in mud, incised deep in the bark of trees—birds and beasts of all kinds but, most often, over and over again, the little cat with her sharp face and swollen body, as he had first seen her.

Near his old hiding-place by the pool, he scooped mud in his hands and made solid forms, shapes he could hold. These satisfied him better than the flat pictures could though they were not more permanent. They cracked apart in the sun's heat but they were good to make—and now Matthew's eyes learned from his hands. Sitting near the lair with his back against a tree, he learned to carve while the kittens played about his feet, testing their teeth and claws upon each other. Their movement was beyond his skill but he made an image of their mother lying quiet, asleep, her chin on her paws.

The days shortened toward autumn. The smells of the forest changed, and the colours changed too. Berries reddened and plumped out, filled with sweetness. The cat went back to her hunting and took the kittens with her, the wild claimed them. When Matthew was sure she would not come back he left the wooden cat to take her place. He was alone again but with this great difference. His solitude was no longer so hard a thing to bear—he had become a maker.

It was his secret and precious to him—but it was soon found out. A small lad, sent with the pigs to forage for acorns, saw Matthew at his whittling and spread the story round the village that the Devil's get was working at magic in the greenwood, making images and muttering to himself. Then Bran, the blacksmith's son, a great brawny lout, went into the wood to catch him at it. The Devil would be afeared to tangle with *him*, he said.

Matthew turned to run, trying to hide the piece of root he was carving but Bran, for all his size and weight, was nimble-footed and quickly caught him, twisting his arm until Matthew let the root fall into his hand.

Whatever Bran had expected to see, it was not this. He looked at the root and looked again, and then at Matthew who stood by with his head bowed.

'What does it mean?' he asked, tracing the line of it with his thick forefinger.

Matthew had never thought of his occupation in terms of meaning. A thing was what it was and meant no more than that; whatever in its nature could not be understood at once would be revealed in time. Only ideas had to have meanings.

'It is a snake,' he said. 'And that is a mouse curled in the last coil of the serpent's tail. The mouse is asleep.'

'Why this?' asked Bran again. He could see well enough what was represented there, but the thought of it disturbed him. Such a state of trust between a serpent and a mouse could not exist . . .

Matthew shrugged. 'The shapes were there in the shape of the root. Nothing more.'

'And *you* made it?'

'And other things,' said Matthew. He saw that Bran was looking at him in a new way, almost with respect, and he brought out other carvings to show. He strutted like a cockerel, he felt the cockerel's voice swell in his throat. And Bran, who was strong enough to swing the blacksmith's great hammer, squatted on the ground and admired all he saw.

This is friendship, Matthew thought, and it is an easy thing— easy as water is to a fish, as air to a bird. But it was not friendship. The quality of the light changed—from bright to dim almost in the space of a breath—and Bran's face darkened too. The sudden dusk had made him afraid and fear made him dangerous. He put his mouth close to Matthew's ear and whispered, 'Who taught you this?'

'Why, I taught myself,' Matthew said, and laughed because the pleasure of friendship and its warmth was still with him. But Bran's hand was on his shoulder, the hard strong fingers digging into his flesh so that he winced.

'I taught myself,' Matthew said again, and Bran struck him, not with his full strength but sufficient to make him reel and cry out.

'That is a lie,' said Bran. 'How can a person teach himself what he does not first know? And if he knows, what need has he of teaching?'

'No one taught me,' said Matthew.

'The Devil taught you,' said Bran and spat to his left to avert the ill luck that might follow. It is a risky thing to mention the Devil aloud in wooded places. 'Admit it.'

Matthew looked at his hands. He could not say whence came their skill—perhaps Bran had guessed right and the Devil was in it somewhere, but there was no way of knowing truly. He sighed.

'There was a wild cat,' he said. 'I loved her and wanted to make her image. I tried and it was no good. I tried again and it was better. I look at things and I make them. There is no more.'

'It is enough,' said Bran. 'Your father whispers in your head and guides your hands. That is why you make such unlikely things—a mouse asleep in a snake's coils—can you say that you saw that and copied it?'

He went back to the village and told what he had seen, making a great thing of the telling.

Mistress Hodge said, 'Eh! it was an ill time when my goodman brought him in from the cold, and so I told him—but a man must always know better! Now surely we will all be punished for nurturing the Devil's child . . .'

The priest said he would not permit such talk. Moreover he remembered naming the boy and was unwilling, now, to let the Devil have him.

Bran told again about the snake Matthew had made. 'He said he had seen it with his own eyes. He looks at things and makes them, and this was one. A mouse and a snake asleep together.'

'What Christian ever heard of such a thing?' cried Mistress Hodge.

Nonetheless the priest insisted that he would see for himself. The good Lord would protect him from all evil, he told his flock.

Matthew and the priest had little knowledge of each other. They had not met since the day when the priest had claimed the child for his church, and Matthew grew up in ignorance of all that this same church offered in the way of comfort and salvation. It was something he would not have understood, a mystery to add to those other unsolved mysteries he had set aside. He had, indeed, listened at the church door once but got no good from it—a mumbling of words less meaningful than the babble of the stream over stones. Yet when the priest found him, beckoned and said, 'Come, my boy!' Matthew went with him.

The old man was not at ease in the woods. Branches snatched at his long gown, brambles tore it and burs clung. He made a great business of his progress too, stopping often to wipe his brow with his sleeve, and to draw breath. Yet he led the way and Matthew, who knew every path in the wood by heart, followed.

At first he followed without thinking. In his early dealings with the village, scant as they were, he had learned obedience; he had learned to come and go as he was ordered because, if he were not quick to obey, he was beaten. In this way he had followed the priest, simply because he was bidden. Then, suddenly, Matthew remembered something that made him afraid. He guessed that they were going to the church and he remembered that, if the Devil were his father, the church—being the house of God—was no place for him. God and the Devil, so he had heard, were mortal enemies. It was only right that the priest should know.

Matthew slid down a little bank at a twist of the path and appeared suddenly before the priest, like a goblin conjured out of the air.

'Sir,' he said, stammering as though it were Bran he faced, and not a breathless, trembling old man. 'Sir, I cannot go with you. The Devil is my father, they say, and I cannot go with you.'

But the old priest merely smiled and answered that indeed he had heard such things said, but for his part he did not think them true. Matthew liked his smile and decided he might trust him, even as far as the church.

It was a small place and poor, a stone room with lime-washed walls and a cracked bell hanging outside under a roof of its own. The priest took my hand

and overcame my reluctance to enter. The air struck very cold and the light was dim. I have seen many great churches since and have lost my fear of them—but that first time I shall never forget. Even now, when I close my eyes, memory brings it back to me complete. There was a low table at one end, with a cloth over it, and a long bench against one wall. We sat together on the bench, the priest and I, and watched motes of dust dance in the sunlight that fell in two long beams from the narrow windows set high in the opposite wall . . .

The priest sat beside Matthew, not touching him, wondering how best to win his confidence. He wanted the boy to talk, to ask questions, to say what he thought, felt, knew; he wanted him to come, awake, into the fold of the church and awareness of God— and he knew neither how to begin nor what to offer. At last he said, 'Well, boy, I hear you are a maker.'

Matthew was held speechless between fear and trust. He was unable to guess what the priest wanted of him, sure that he must have done some wrong and was brought here for punishment—yet the old man's voice was tender, he did not seem angry. Matthew concentrated his gaze on the slit of sky he could see through the window and waited for the priest to speak again.

'It is a gift of God, Matthew, to be used for his eternal glory. Do you understand what that means?'

Children often find it hard to admit their ignorance. Matthew did not understand—but he nodded.

'What do you make?'

'Birds and beasts,' said Matthew, and his hand closed on the frog he had lately made and still carried with him safe in a knot of his ragged tunic. 'Sometimes leaves and flowers, but beasts most often—'

'Have you ever carved a man?'

The boy shook his head. Just as one learns something by carving it, so also one learns to carve well what one knows best. Matthew knew no men.

The priest took him by the shoulders and drew him down the church, to stand before the table.

'Look,' he commanded. And Matthew raised his eyes.

Behind and above the table there hung a man, the carving of a man. He was naked, except for a folded cloth about his loins, and emaciated. His belly was a dark hollow below the sharp jut of his ribs, and his outspread arms, nailed by the hands to a cross-piece of wood, were no more than sinew and bone. The body hung from those pierced hands and its weight dragged on them, the shoulders dislocated. His head had dropped forward so that the chin rested on his breast but the eyes were open and the mouth twisted in agony that had no end. Not even death, when it should come, could put a stop to such anguish as that.

I was not a stranger to pain. I had seen snared rabbits often enough, and what remains from a fox's kill. For all their beauty, the woods have never been a gentle place. But this, that the priest showed me, was something worse. Looking, I lost my innocence.

'Could you make such a carving as that?' the priest asked him. And Matthew looked again, this time with a critical eye, following the grain of the wood, seeing the marks of the maker's tool, where it had gouged too deep or not deep enough, feeling with his mind's hands the shape of the figure, until his own hands itched to begin. If his heart warned him of danger, he did not heed it.

'I have never carved a man,' he said, 'nor anything big.' He showed the frog, small enough to hold in the hollow of his palm, and the old man took it, caressing it with his thumb as he turned it about. Matthew liked the way he held it as, a little earlier, he had liked his smile.

Then the priest asked if he had ever attempted a man and Matthew told him that he had only his knife to work with, and the blade had been whetted so often it was almost worn away.

'It was never a good blade at best,' he said. ''Twould take the Devil's own skill to carve a man with that.'

The priest suppressed a laugh and Matthew wondered what he had said to make him merry. Also he was offended, for his words had been seriously spoken, after thought.

'Will you try?' said the priest. 'If I give you wood and the tools you need, and a place to work in, and food and drink to sustain you, will you carve me a man?'

I am wiser now and I know what temptation is, that it comes in many guises and that it is always something to resist, but in those days I was a fool.

'Give me all those things,' said Matthew, throwing back his head to look directly in the priest's eyes, 'and I will carve you a man that will climb down from his cross and walk.'

The priest then took him to a hut built against the side of his house, behind the church, and showed him where everything was set ready for his use.

'*My* use?' Matthew asked, not believing. It seemed unlikely, even to his credulity, that a priest should have such things by him, to give away as he wished.

'There was a man lived here once,' the priest said. He tried to explain the man, but nothing came to mind beyond a picture of strong, scarred hands and the sound of a voice. 'A skilful carver in wood. This hut was his, this bench, this whetstone and the tools . . .'

It was he who made the dying man, Matthew thought.

'Where is he now?'

The priest walked to the doorway and stood, looking away across the fields. The harvest was all gathered in and the ground looked dark and barren, as though nothing had ever grown there. He remembered then that the woodcarver had been a golden man, like the harvest, and that when he went, the whole world grew dark for a little while, and very quiet and very empty.

'Who knows?' he said. 'No one saw him go. He had left work unfinished and, because of that, I thought he would come back . . . It is something I shall never understand.'

It was that same winter, he remembered, that old Hodge had found the child in the snow and brought him home. A bitter, black winter full of loss.

'I greased his tools and wrapped them so they would not rust. They are all here.'

There were so many tools—Matthew had not thought so many tools could be. He went from one to another, lifting them, feeling their weight and balance, testing their sharp edges against his skin.

'He is surely dead now,' the priest mused, waiting for grief to prick.

Matthew put down the rasp he was holding, and backed away from it. He knew it was unlucky to handle a dead man's belongings without first appeasing his ghost and he thought it strange that the priest, reckoned a wise man, should not know this too. He tried to explain it to him but the priest would not understand and kept repeating, 'It cannot matter now. He is dead.'

Matthew put his hands to his ears and ran away, back to the woods where he might be safe from the dead man's things. He had always been safe in the woods, he should have stayed there. He should not have trusted the priest . . .

And now all was changed. The beasts who had been his friends ran from his approach and hid themselves as though he were an enemy. The smell of the church, like dust and candle-wax, was on his clothes, on his skin, and he could no longer go among them as their brother. There was no place left for him but the hut by the priest's house.

So there I went, very fearfully and dragging my feet—until I was near enough to feel the pull of the craftsman's tools . . . That old priest, a good and simple man, had taught me covetousness and, for the greater glory of his god, had sacrificed my innocence. Now, as I neared his house, with every step I took, my mind awakened a little more, setting its seal on my imagination. I, who had made beasts with great love in my hands and heart, would make a man.

And I had no love for men.

The priest kept his word, he gave Matthew food and drink, straw to lie on and a blanket to cover him at night. He gave thought to the boy's soul too, speaking to him of God and the holy angels, and of God's son who came to save the world—none of which Matthew understood. Indeed, talk of the Resurrection alarmed rather than consoled him for he did not forget how the dead badger had looked after three days. Christmas he liked because of the shepherds and the inn-yard and the beasts, but Eastertide filled him with dread and he was always glad when it was over and he could look forward to Pentecost again, with its tongues of flame leaping from the sky, and all the people running from their houses into the street.

Matthew's skill increased. He carved the man the priest wanted—and the village people, who had cared so little for his infant misery, were amazed by it and declared his work a glory.

'And 'twas my man brung him home that winter,' Hodge's goodwife reminded them. 'Wi'out Hodge, he'd 'a shrammed o' cold.' No one denied it, nor their own generous part in the boy's rearing.

'He'll bless 'ee for it,' they said. 'And us too. God have surely touched his hands.'

They did not speak of the Devil any more—at least, not in Matthew's hearing. The priest had seen to that. But they were still wary and kept their distance. They had always thought him strange and certainly he was strange to them still—but here he had his own place and condition—he was Matthew who carved beasts and men, the priest had his governing. It was not so easy to drive him away.

A fat monk, riding from the Abbey to collect his Abbot's dues, took him aside and told him with great solemnity that God had taught him a hallowed mystery and that he must use his gift humbly, with thankfulness. By then Matthew had learned to dissemble when it suited him and he gave the monk an answer calculated to please, though he knew well that this great and holy mystery had been shown him, not by God, but by a fierce pregnant cat, wild and alone, and that, for her sake, he would use his gift with pride.

When the monk had gone his way with laden saddle-bags, Matthew made a cruel little image of him astride his short-legged jennet—the monk with plump-jowled face and pious, upturned eyes, his bulk dwarfing the modest, over-burdened beast. He chuckled, making it, and even the priest laughed—though he turned the laugh into a cough and almost choked on it. After that he was very quiet and looked for a long time into the fire, not speaking.

A month or two after this, the priest took Matthew with him to a distant town where a cathedral was being raised. He had some private business to occupy him, he said, and left the boy by himself to watch the masons and stonecarvers at work in a place of soaring walls and pillars that were like the trunks of trees but stone—a place of noise and light and dust and activity, all directed to one single purpose . . .

He must have been a great nuisance to the workmen that day, constantly underfoot, running from the blacksmith's forge to the place where carpenters were assembling trusses for the scaffolding, and back again, staying to watch the carvers shaping downspouts that would carry water from the gutters on the roof, begging to be allowed to carry a hod or steady a load. More than once he missed by a hair's breadth having his brains scattered by a mighty block of stone swinging in its tackle, and only grinned when the mason leaned down to curse him as he skipped to safety.

At length the priest came back and fetched Matthew away to the lodging-house where he had reserved a corner for them in the common straw. His day had gone well—so much was obvious from the pleased and secret air he had about him—and that his business had somehow concerned the boy was obvious too from the way he kept glancing sideways at him and smiling, straightening his face again whenever he saw Matthew looking. But though Matthew plagued him with questions, and coaxed, and offered bribes of good behaviour, he would not say one word about his day, except, 'Later, boy. Time enough.' Until Matthew grew tired of asking and sulked instead.

So Matthew ate his supper with a show of indifference and as great an appetite as though there were nothing momentous brewing. To be eating salt beef and barley broth at a long table among pedlars and pilgrims, while all the bells of all the churches in the town clamoured all around and overhead, might have been an everyday event in his young life, he so disdained it.

The priest ate little. His face looked sad now, rather than joyful. The excitement and pleasures of the day had taken a severe toll of his strength, and he began to doubt the wisdom of what he had done. His head acknowledged it right, but his heart failed him— and it had always been the wisdom of the heart he trusted.

'Matthew,' he said. 'I am growing old now, and you are still a boy—' No, that was not what he meant. He cleared his throat and tried again.

'I have thought a great deal about your future . . .' That was better. Youth looked to the future, he knew.

Matthew waited. He was used to his master's slow and wandering speech and did not mind it. There was always something to watch—a dog scratching, a duck upended in the millstream, a rat's bright eyes in the shadows of the woodpile—and here there was even more. A man at the far end of the table had a cage of singing birds for sale; two men with red faces were arguing hotly about a piece of land; the lodging-house cat crept, low on her belly, her haunches wriggling, toward the birds . . . It was some time before the priest managed to say what he had to say, he made so many starts and stumbles, but the gist was clear. He had, that very day, enrolled the boy as a *famulus* in the charge of a master-mason, one Jacques Thibaud, a man of good living and high reputation. Then the words came.

'You will learn to dress stone, mix mortar and care for the mason's tools. Then, if you serve him well, he will take you as apprentice and teach you the craft . . . in time you will become a master-mason yourself. Why, Matthew, you will travel the world, enriching it everywhere with noble buildings, praising God every day with the skill of your hands . . .' Tears welled from his eyes, too fast to staunch. He let them flow. Matthew, himself, was close to weeping.

'You planned all this for *me*?'

'Since the first day . . . I have your frog still . . .' He brought out the small beast Matthew had once given him and long-since forgotten, and put it on the table between them. Matthew looked at it and thought it a poor, rough piece of work, not worth keeping for a day. Yet this old man had carried it for a year or more and saw no fault in it—how could he bear to let its maker go?

'You are sending me away.' It was an accusation. Matthew had known once what it was to be rejected—now he was to be rejected again.

'For the greater glory of God,' said the priest and put his hand on the boy's head in a gesture that was, at the same time, a renunciation of his personal claim on him and a blessing. This is the second person I have loved, he told his god. The first you sent away from me, this one I give you. Take care of him.

I knew then that I wanted to carve stone more than I wanted anything in life, that I needed to breathe stone-dust more than I needed air—and he knew it too, putting the means in my hand. But I accused him of wanting to be rid of me. I have hoped since that he was not too much pained by my response. Almost at once I thanked him and kissed his hands, but I should have done that at first. The 'almost' remains with me, and hurts still. The next day he presented me to Master Thibaud at the masons' lodge and left me there—for the greater glory of God. I never saw him again.

Matthew served Jacques Thibaud for seven years; the lodge was his home; the brothers and wardens, his family. His days were as ordered as those of a monk, from sun-up when he was roused from sleep by the music of a hammer striking stone till evening when he put down his tools and returned to the lodge for supper. And his whole life was bound up with the cathedral which rose—stone upon stone, arch, buttress and pinnacle—toward completion. Master Thibaud was a good man to serve, a patient teacher as ready to give praise where it was earned as he was to punish a fault known and uncorrected. He was respected even by the clergy who employed him, and the least of the day-labourers revered him as though he were the Pope. The old priest had done well by Matthew when he chose a new master for him.

The seven years passed and Matthew was admitted to the

degree of bachelor of the craft. He wrote his thesis on building, illustrated it in stone, and finally was raised to the rank of master. On that day he gave a feast for his fellow masons, with beef and capons and Rhenish wine, as much as they could hold—and, as his brothers pledged him, and he them, Matthew put his hand on the carved oak of his chair, confident of its reality, while he remembered that he was the same Matthew, the Devil's by-blow, who had been driven, hungry, from door to door. It was this same I, he thought, who never received a gift from any man before the priest gave me my tools, who stands here now in a fine, woollen gown, making gifts of gloves to the wardens of my lodge, and he was filled with pride.

In those seven years he had grown to be a man, a master-craftsman with hands strong enough and hard enough to wield the hammers and mallets of his trade, yet delicate enough to trace plans and make drawings. He could read well and write in a fair, clerkly hand, and he knew how to bear himself with dignity.

Yet, for all that, he had not fulfilled his old vow, his boast that he would make a man so true he would climb down from his cross and walk. And it rankled.

He made a Christ in majesty for the tympanum above the south entrance, a smiling Christ with rabbits peering from the folds of his robe, and a bird in his lap. This was praised by the whole town, coming singly and in groups to see it; some even called it one of the wonders of the world, which was too great a praise, Matthew thought, and it troubled him deeply for, in his own eyes, it was no more than a piece of stone with the marks of his chisel on it.

He made a man's head surrounded by a wreath of leaves, the face dappled with shadows in such a way that he was like some old vanquished god of the forest, half tree, half man—but it was less to Matthew than the small wooden cat he had once hidden among roots in an earthy hollow.

Nothing he made had the power to satisfy him. He grew morose and carved monsters and devils to hide the mouths of rain-spouts high on the buttresses. He hated his own hands till they shook with his hatred.

Master Thibaud warned him. He had seen it all before, he said, it was a much travelled road—and it led nowhere.

They were standing in a side-chapel in the light of a coloured window given by the guild of weavers. Above them, bow-legged little men, outlined sharply in lead, cut their cloth from the loom, baled it and offered it to Saint Mary Magdalene. The sun, slanting through the glass, stained Master Thibaud's hands with blue and yellow.

'No man can create more than the shadow of reality,' he said. 'The higher he strives, the closer he approaches his own truth, but God—in the wisdom we cannot question—has set a limit to the height a man may scale. To go beyond that limit is to fall into sin. *Hubris*, Matthew, the sin of Lucifer. The creation of life is God's prerogative.'

'At least it was a sin worth losing Heaven for,' said Matthew. 'I want perfection.'

'Well,' said Master Thibaud, uneasy between praise and dis-approval, 'it is a good hunger. You should want nothing less.' Then he let his voice grow stern again. 'But understand your limit, Matthew, accept it. Make what is in your power to make—and leave the rest to God. Or you will end by making nothing.'

Thibaud was right, there was no gainsaying it, but as it was not advice Matthew wanted to hear, he packed his tools and took to the road, secure in the knowledge that, as long as bishops and prelates vied with each other in building, glorifying themselves as much as the God they professed to serve, he would never lack for work when he needed it. Meanwhile, there was money in his pouch; he was not compelled by the bare necessity which drives a man from one task to the next. He could take his time, following any road that caught his fancy.

Yet I had no pleasure in my travelling. My anger made me blind to much that I should have seen and stored away—patterns of leaf and branch, curled fronds of ferns, the splayed roots of old trees laid bare. I turned my face from these, grudging them their substance, because they were, so I was told, God's work—and whatever God made, I swore, I could make too, in stone, and better. And God paid me back, coin for coin, in misery.

Neither noticing where he went nor much caring, Matthew passed through villages, markets and towns, some thriving, expanding into cities, some declining almost to ruin but, to him, each one as like the others as are matched beads on a chain. Yet he was not quite indifferent. He knew he lacked something and that, once he found it, all would be well with him again. So he looked for signs in the faces of those he met, hoping he would recognize that which he missed in himself. But he saw only his own fears reflected, thrown back at him from features other than his but clearly the same fears, the same disillusionment.

Sometimes he travelled in company, for the sake of talk, but his own talk was so uneasy it silenced that of others. 'What is truth?' he would ask, suddenly, his question interrupting a rambling tale, stopping the teller short as though he were accused of lying. Or 'But *who* made God?' asked with such fierceness and sincerity that it could not be counted blasphemy, even by a bishop.

In one town he found himself caught up in a wedding party and carried along to the feast by the bride's father, rather drunk and garrulous, glad to have rid himself of yet another daughter. He had nine, he said, and this was only the fifth to be given away, which meant four more husbands to find and money was getting short.

'I'll have to keep the youngest by me, for there'll be nothing left by then,' he confided. 'And, to be honest with you, she's a plain, bad-tempered girl . . .'

This description suited the bride as well, Matthew thought, but the groom seemed well-satisfied and scattered coins for the children as liberally as a king would, on the way from his crowning.

Until then Matthew had given little thought to marriage. While his work progressed, he had wanted nothing else, and when it went badly, he was, he knew, so ill-tempered no wife would endure him long. Yet marriage was reckoned a good state. Though most husbands complained of their freedom docked like a dog's tail, leaving them nothing to wag, they had more compensations than loss, he suspected, and the pleasure of having a son to teach would surely make up for a world of scolding inconvenience . . .

In this frame of mind, he came to a city where a duke was visiting, with a great train of lesser lords and knights and men-at-arms filling up all the houses and making accommodation both costly and hard to find. Matthew saw him riding by in the evening, his new-wed duchess beside him on a mare that looked as gentle as

(26)

she did, and he took off his dusty cap to them, thinking, 'There goes a happy man.'

But he was wrong, it seemed.

The innkeeper told him the duke's story and there was a thread of sadness in it. The pretty duchess had been a girl chance-met at the roadside—she stood back to let the horsemen pass, the duke looked at her, was enslaved by what he saw, and married her.

'Princess or peasant, who can tell? Who knows? For she's dumb as a post, God help her—'

He sighed a gust of stale breath, and his eyes were moist.

'I've never thought speechlessness so bad a thing in a woman,' said a man with a wall-eye, who was standing near.

Matthew nodded, sagely, appearing to agree with both.

'It's a courtly tale,' he said. 'The sort of tale that lords and ladies delight in when the weather's bad and time heavy on their hands. But it would take a limner's brush to tell it to perfection—and that's too fine an art for my taste.'

'Indeed?' said the innkeeper, gauging with precise exactness Matthew's capacity for more ale and the weight of his purse. A good spender must be humoured.

Matthew drank again and tried to tell the fellow that, though he did not despise the illuminator's craft, he himself needed something more—the opposing weight of hard, obdurate stone, something he could wrestle with and which would resist him. But his belly was awash with ale and the fumes of it rose thick as fog in his head, he wished the innkeeper would stand still in one place and not advance and recede in so uncertain a manner.

'A limner's brush . . .' he repeated, with a belch that took him by surprise. 'It's an art invented to make you smile . . .'

The innkeeper smiled then, as though obediently, and for some reason Matthew could not fathom, the smile angered him.

'Yet God laboured for six days,' he said. 'God laboured for six days and created man—a puny, naked thing. Forked like a mandrake. Venomous as serpent's spittle. And heir to every sorrow and glory of the world. Did God smile?' he asked, his voice rising. 'Did God *smile* when he saw the man that he had made?'

Embarrassed by such terrible earnestness, the innkeeper backed away, and Matthew banged his ale-pot on the table so that the dark brew frothed over. It was important to him that the innkeeper should understand, that the wall-eyed man should understand, that every man in the room should understand.

'Aye,' he shouted. 'God smiled. For he'd breathed a mind and soul into the thing, and given it a thumb that could grasp a mallet. Adam did not need Eve to tempt him. That had been done already—and by God himself!'

Then he put his head in his arms, all among the ale-pots and puddles, and wept.

The next day he left the city and went on, with an aching head and a sour taste in his mouth. The sky was grey and the wind bitterly cold, with no thought of summer in it. That night he slept, fitfully, in the open, and thanked Saint Thomas, the patron of stone-workers, that at least the rain held off. But it did not hold off for long—Matthew had not been more than an hour on his way before he was drenched and shivering, desperate for any sort of cover. Then Saint Thomas had pity on him. A comfortable widow let him dry his clothes in front of her fire and he repaired two wooden bench-ends for her in return for a meal or two and the shelter of her barn.

To farmers and travellers, both, weather is a fickle mistress. After a day and a night of rain came drought, a punishing sun in a sky that was like white metal, and Matthew would have given half of what was left in his purse to see the clouds again.

A hot day and a relentless thirst. Even the grasses at the side of the road and between the wheel-ruts had a parched and brittle look. The earth was baked dry. The weight of my precious tools—my mallets and chisels and gouges— banged on my shoulders and the heat from the leather sling in which I carried them seared my back even through the thickness of my tunic. I had a strange feeling that I was the only man left alive in a burning world and that I too would die and the world be reduced to cinders. I thought of the streams and rivers drying up, one after another, and the lakes and seas and the uncharted oceans, great ships stranded, dry, salt-silvered, manned by the bones of sailors drowned in too much air . . .

It was then that I came to the goose-girl's hut.

Further back, below the dip of a hill, I had passed a tidy farm with outbuildings where, surely, I would have been given water—but I had pressed on. The farm had registered on my eye, but not in my mind. Now I turned aside and stepped onto the goose-cropped green.

Geese are birds with a strong sense of territory, they know what is their own and will defend it to the last feather. When an exhausted stranger stepped onto their green, Gerda's big grey gander challenged him at once, striking at his legs with his hard beak and making a great strident noise of defiance. Gerda heard the fuss and came hurrying at once to rescue whoever had been so courageous or so desperate as to trespass on her land with Barney there to protect it, and all the geese—except Barney, who stayed on guard—ran to her, dishevelled with indignation and protesting as loudly as he.

'Barney, you girt fool,' she scolded, clapping her hands at him. 'When will 'ee learn to give strangers a kindlier welcome?'

And then she smiled at Matthew, to put him at his ease.

Women had smiled at him before—and some had been fine women in silk gowns, marriage-rings on their fingers—but when this woman smiled, it seemed to Matthew like the coming of spring after a cruel winter. He would have sworn that flowers opened in the grass round her bare feet, and staked his life on it.

But Gerda, looking at Matthew, saw him more plainly—a man of low stature, scarcely taller than herself, very travel-stained and weary, yet with a look of authority not often encountered in a man dressed like a peasant. She did not think him particularly ugly, nor very handsome; rating honesty above any sort of beauty, she could barely tell one extreme from the other, and she smiled, not in invitation but because her friendliness embraced everyone—and because she felt bound to make up for Barney's discourtesy.

'I came to beg a drink from your well,' he said. 'Not to intrude on your privacy. Your gander credits me with worse motives, so call him off, lady, and I'll go my way.'

'No. I can give 'ee water,' she said. 'Barney, scoot!' The gander huffed away, grumbling, and Gerda led Matthew to her well behind the house, where she drew water for him. She was a little flustered, almost vexed, at being addressed as 'lady', as though she were someone in a fairy tale and not her own goose-girl self but, she decided, these must be city manners and she would prove equal to them, let him see.

'Don't mind Barney,' she said. 'You can rest if you want.' And she sat beside him in the shade of the tall elm by the well, spreading her skirt to hide her feet, which she was sure a lady would not show. Barney reappeared to march him to the road again, but

Gerda frowned at him and bade him be still and quiet. She wanted to hear Matthew's story.

'Have you travelled far?' she asked him.

As he had kept no tally of the days, he could not tell her, so he spoke instead of his life and of his work as a master-mason. Perhaps he boasted a little, for the gander shrugged out his wings and made a noise that was unmistakably derisive. Matthew could have wrung his neck and roasted him without a qualm but Gerda laughed and put her arms round the bird, closing his beak with one hand, ruffling the feathers of his breast with the other.

Her skin was like honey and her hands were grimed from work in her vegetable patch. I should never have called her 'lady'—she was something so much better than that.

She told him her name but there was nothing she could say about her life, the days passed without excitement. She reared geese and cared for them; in return, they protected her.

'They need not disturb themselves about me,' said Matthew, for the gander's hearing. 'I am a maker, not a spoiler.'

He wondered if she had ever seen her face reflected, if she knew how she looked, with her wide high cheekbones and freckled skin. Her eyes were blue, almost the colour of cornflowers, and her teeth were very white. No, she is not strictly beautiful, thought Matthew, yet she is beautiful to me.

'You must be very happy,' he said. There was a sort of arrogance in his belief that everyone must be happy except himself.

'I've seen naught of the world,' she said. 'I've not been further than the farm below the field one way, and the market town in the other. I've never been to the city—'

'It's only a place,' Matthew told her. 'High buildings and narrow streets. The houses bow to each other across the thoroughfares—oh, very stately, but the sky is quite shut out. You'd not be able to breathe there, Gerda, and a goose would have no worth at all except in a dish on a merchant's table. You and your Barney are better where you are.'

'I'm not quite a fool,' she said, hotly. 'There's many folk use this road, both going to the city and coming back from it. I speak to

(31)

them when they stop, and they tell me about it. What's more,' she insisted, 'the duke has a house there. Would *he* choose a place where there's no air to breathe? And I've heard there's a great square all paved with stones like the floor o' the manor house—but open to the sky. And the duke's house is three times as big as a church, the walls hung wi' patterned silk, richer than a lady's gown. There's water there too, where they've cut a path for the river to flow round the city—and there are swans on it. If you say otherwise, then it's your own sourness talking.'

She was very simple and Matthew loved her for it. She clasped her strong, sensible hands together and closed her eyes the better to see the pictures her words conjured. Matthew remembered the beggars who sat from morning till night in the great square that was paved like the floor of a manor house—old soldiers crippled from the wars, simpletons, rogues—and the stink from the open gutters. But he said, 'You are right. There are such wonders to be seen in the city that I am jealous of them.'

Then, because he wanted to please her, he told her of the merchants' houses that were as fine as palaces, and of the merchants' wives who prinked and pranced, aping their betters, and had servants to wait on them, and how these same servants were so proud of their masters' wealth that they looked down on the servants of other, lesser men. He told her of feasts and processions and holy days, of crowds gathered to hear the crusade preached or to see a princess wed. His imagination made up for what his experience lacked, and he talked until the sun dropped low in the sky.

Gerda sighed deeply, pleasure mingled with regret; she would never see these things for herself but it was good to hear of them. And Barney was growing restless. It was one thing to give water to a thirsty man, quite another to waste a day in listening to his tall tales. He tapped her foot to remind her that life was too serious a matter to spend in idleness. It was time for Matthew to give thought to his going.

The goose-girl rose to wish him God-speed, and they stood together for a moment, looking at the sky which promised another blistering day ahead. The rooks were making a huge fuss in the elm's high branches, like angry clerics arguing a point of law.

Then, 'Look!' cried Gerda, and pointed.

Eleven swans were flying from the east, their wings beating in unison, rising and falling in the same slow rhythm, and it seemed to Matthew as though they dragged the blanket of the dark behind them, it followed so quickly on their passing. Barney stretched his long neck and threatened them, shouting abuse at the sky, but the swans would not have heard him. And if they had heard, they would not have cared.

Before many more weeks had gone by, the lightness of Matthew's purse made it necessary for him to find employment again and he knocked at the door of a lodge in a city very like the one he had left. His reputation as a stonecarver had preceded him and the two fellow-masons who welcomed him to the lodge had also been apprentices of Jacques Thibaud—though before Matthew's time—and had worked on the same cathedral. They were glad to introduce him to the master in charge of building, and to vouch for him, so Matthew was engaged at once to carve figures for the north and west portals, with the certainty of other work to come. The travelling had eased him and steadied his hands.

Matthew picked up his life again almost where he had left it. He carved saints and angels, prophets and priests and kings—and for a long time he was content. The master was delighted, he told Matthew that the Dean admired his work so much he wanted a Virgin from him, to stand in the Lady Chapel the duke had promised to endow—it was to be the finest chapel in Christendom, the lightest, the most airy, the most richly furnished. Matthew should consider himself greatly honoured, it was rarely that such a commission fell to so young a man. He knew it, and was as proud as he had been on the day he showed the serpent carving to young Bran, the blacksmith's son. He went to the quarry and chose his stone, marking it for his use and giving orders for its transporting to the city . . .

But then, between one day and the next, the old hunger came again, the urge to make something that would live and breathe, that would combine in walking stone the passion and intelligence of man with the innocence of a beast. And it would not be satisfied.

There was a gap between his intention and his hands—and it widened. Where he should have carved a portrait of the founding bishop carrying a model of his church and gazing into the future, Matthew made instead the figure of a mitred ass beating a hand-drum and grinning over its shoulder. Someone else must see to the bishop . . .

'Dear God,' said Matthew. 'There are enough masons here to carve an avenue of bishops from this city to Rome. Why plague me with it?' He would quarrel with anyone who approached him, whether apprentice or master or the Dean himself—but he still worked. Then he stopped working, answered only the most direct of questions, and sat apart from the communal meals. He was clamped in misery.

My lodge-brothers were very patient, I remember. They left me alone to recover in my own way and in my own time, which is always best. Perhaps they were afraid of me too, thinking of the story we had all heard, of a mason in Rouen who killed an apprentice whose rose-window was finer than his. That is a shuddering tale—but a true one. I think that, even at my worst, I would never have gone so far . . . good work is surely a pleasure in itself, not one to excite envy in a fellow-craftsman. Yet how could my brothers know this when I sat with such a brooding face and such restless hands?

I shall never know how many days or weeks I lost for, where there is no sense or reason, there is no time. One hour was like the next and identical with the one preceding it. I found it hard even to distinguish between noon and dusk.

But the mind, left to itself, heals itself. One night Matthew found himself standing at the massive south door of the cathedral, not knowing how he came to be there, whether by chance or design. Apart from a feeling of shock, like that of a sleepwalker suddenly awakened, he had no ill effects from his long sickness—if sickness it could be called; his whole interest had sprung into life again, all his senses heightened as though disuse had made them new.

He watched how the moonlight sharpened the shadows of the carving above the portal and how, when a cloud crossed the moon, the shadows were lost again, as if centuries of years had blunted the bright edges. The moon glided free and there, as before, were the saints in their niches, every feature clear, every fold of their gowns precise and true. And permanent. For the space of an hour Matthew stood and watched the play of shadows along the arch as the clouds veiled and unveiled the moon. He opened the door and went in one step from silver light into velvet dark, from silence into sound. No place of worship is ever empty. There are always those who spend their lives in prayer—for the dead, for the King, for the Holy Wars, for the remission of sins. The rise and fall of the voices seemed to Matthew like the fretted tracery of the chantry screen translated into music. The vast interior was filled with echoes.

He borrowed a candle from Saint Thomas and made a round of the church. Dust lay everywhere, but it was not the dust of neglect. Tomorrow it would be scuffed by several dozen pairs of feet, now only Matthew's disturbed it. He felt like a ghost returning to its earthly home and finding nothing changed. He thanked God nothing was changed. There was his block of stone as he had left it, untouched, smooth, marked with his own mark. He held the candle close and looked again, loving it with his eyes, and felt the remembered itching at the base of his thumbs, his hands saying *yes* to it.

I slept deeply that night and wakened refreshed to the sound of the hammer-blow. In this town we still followed the old ways, going in procession to the site and chanting prayers as we went, like so many monks. The bishop insisted that each day must begin devoutly—no matter what other songs we sang at our work—and we were willing to humour him in so small an observance. In another country, not so long ago, a bishop had tried to make the masons clip their hair to the skull and shave their beards, but they stopped work at that and threatened to burn the church rather than obey. It was too great an interference, they said. Compared with such an order, the chanting of prayers was nothing.

So we walked very solemnly on our way to work, as though the very ground we trod was holy—but in the cathedral itself we broke our fast, and no one suggested that our appetite profaned it. We chanted prayers outside the building dedicated to God, but inside it we shouted and made a great clangour and never thought of God at all.

Matthew thought he had forgotten Gerda. And certainly he had forgotten her with the surface part of the mind, the part which occupies itself with the business of living—but a man's memory has wide vaults and somewhere in his there must have lingered the image of a kindly girl surrounded by geese. And it was this image he drew from the heart of his stone—not the Consort and Mother of God the Dean had commissioned, but Our Lady of the Geese, still young and without grief. This was the mother of Christ's childhood, Matthew thought. The cross was not yet even a shadow on the hillside. It was the best time of all, and the one the Church forgot.

⟨✿⟩

The Dean was a man with a yearning toward grandeur. People said it vexed him to be reminded, each year, that his God had been born in a stable, laid in an ox's manger and worshipped by shepherds. It was a fact he tried to ignore, liking better the bright, guiding star and the three kings.

Matthew guessed such a one would not willingly accept the Lady of the Geese for his magnificent chapel—and he prepared to defend his work. Yet there was no question of a simple refusal. The Dean dared not say outright that the work did not suit him for he was paying highly for Matthew's skill and to decry what use was made of it would, by his measure, be an admission of his own lack of judgement.

'Hmm,' he said, cupping his shaven chin in his hand and looking aslant at Matthew to see whether he were offended by such lack of enthusiasm. And 'Hmm,' again. He was in a quandary and Matthew pitied him. None the less, they could not stand for ever, looking at the statue. Something must be resolved.

'A little too much of the peasant?' the Dean said at last, but in a tone which suggested that some trifling alteration might yet make all well. 'I had not envisaged a Lady quite so—rustic.'

Matthew agreed, from his heart. This Lady was obviously a peasant wench, she needed green turf beneath her feet and trees behind her. But surely he was not to blame for finding a goose-girl locked in the stone he had marked and set aside for the Queen of Heaven.

'God guided my hands,' he answered, piously. And it may have been true, for the priests say that not even a sparrow falls without his permission.

But the Dean looked so glum that Matthew relented, clapping him on the shoulder as though he were a friend, not an employer.

'Come, I will make you another,' he said. 'One that will do more credit to your chapel.' Even as he spoke, he saw her clearly—a

(37)

woman somewhat larger than life-sized, crowned, remote, with eyes that looked away toward the end of the world . . .

'It is not that I do not care for this,' the Dean said, and showed his long horse-teeth with relief. 'It is very fine, no doubt. Very fine—but it has no . . .'

'No dignity.' Matthew nodded. 'And what is heart without dignity?'

He started to say, 'Nothing at all.' And then thought better of it. He had a suspicion that I was baiting him but, apart from that brotherly clout, there was nothing improper in my manner toward him. I was going to give him the Lady he wanted, the one he had commissioned, and he had already decided he would not pay for two. The goose-girl Virgin was my loss—but he paid for her in discomfort.

'Rest happy,' Matthew said. 'I will make you a Lady so fine and stately that this entire chapel will have to be refurnished to make it fit for her.'

He meant to do it.

He chose new stone and made a good beginning. The Dean approved the sketches he was shown and came regularly to see how the work progressed—to make certain, too, that Matthew's hands kept to their bargain. The rejected Lady of the Geese was stowed away in a side-chapel and neither the Dean nor Matthew thought of her again.

He was absorbed in his new labour. Each stone is a separate thing, not like any other; each offers its own challenge to the carver. And the carver must accept its challenge and master the stone, but not violently, for that would set its heart against him and make the work ugly. The only derangement in nature is where some damaging force has been at work—and it is so with the sculptor's craft. The true maker must set his will over the will that is in the stone but he must not violate it.

Knowing this, Matthew went to his new work carefully and with respect. He wooed the Lady from her long sleep, cutting her free of the stone that was both her couch and covering until she stood clear of it, a rough shape still, but her own, a woman's shape with head raised and the hands parted in blessing.

'Good,' he said. 'This one has dignity.'

He sculpted the folds of her robe, raised a little to show one sandalled foot set forward, a dignified foot that even the most worldly of men might kiss in pure reverence, with not a profane thought in his head. He modelled the arms resting lightly above the swell of her belly and, with his finest chisels, separated each finger of the long, cold hands . . .

And there he stopped.

He could not *see* the face. The high crown topped a smooth blank oval. Hair curled at each side of it, framed the column of her neck, touched her shoulders—but the Lady remained featureless.

Hour after hour Matthew stood before her, his chisel ready in his hand, and he dared not put it to the stone, he dared not trust its edge. There was other work to be done—he might have veined the Lady's wrists or curved her fingernails—but, being haunted by the empty face and afraid of his own fearfulness, he could not set his mind to it.

And this was something he had not experienced before. The world is full of faces, chance-seen, half-remembered, to be used, the brow from one, the eyes and mouth from another, and he had never hesitated to borrow from life whatever he needed for his stone. He had not even baulked at depicting the face of God. But somehow this dignified Lady defeated him.

He told the Dean he was going away for a little while, to look for a new face for his Lady. He said the same at the lodge and left his swag of tools there as a token of good faith that he would return—but he did not know whether he meant to return or not. The future seemed as blank as the space below the Lady's crown, and as impossible to fill.

A boy had held a dead badger in his hands and wondered about life and death—that had been the start of everything. If he went back there, he thought, to that place, that time, that exact moment, he might find the answer. After all, that boy—himself—who had scarcely known his own name, had known who he was, which was something Matthew no longer knew. But with that boy's knowledge, thought Matthew, and *my* skill, we may yet make something that God will envy, something more perfect than a man.

He took what money he had saved and went across the river.

The watchman on the bridge, an old friend, greeted him and kept him talking a while. This man had troubles too and had often sympathised with Matthew's, though each privately thought the other made a great broil of very little. The watchman considered Matthew touched in the head, and Matthew wondered why any man should fret himself over a daughter and, since it seemed all men did so, why they should confide in him, who had neither wife nor daughter of his own.

Now the watchman said, 'That girl's the joy and sorrow of my life. She keeps my house spotless, her bread is the best in the town, she never raises her voice in irritation, she is—'

'A pearl beyond price,' said Matthew. 'A good wife for a fortunate man. She'll never lack for suitors.'

But this was the very pivot of the problem. The girl was something of a beauty, a good girl, a sad girl whose one desire was to be a nun.

'There's a dozen hot for her,' said her father, bitterly. 'And one's a decent mercer with a shop of his own—and two apprentices. She'd want for nothing. He'd wed her in her shift and ask no marriage-piece at all—but she'll have none of him. It's the Church she's set her heart on—and Christ, it seems, won't take her without a dowry . . .'

Had he been a less likeable man I might have laughed, though it is true my laughter would have had a hollow ring. The preachers are fond of telling us that God is not mocked—yet God mocks man with every breath he takes. We live in an imperfect world. No man is happy. Everything is flawed.

Matthew could say nothing that would console him so he reminded him again of the Dean who had only a faceless Virgin to set in his Lady Chapel and had paid good money for her.

'That can be put right,' the watchman said. 'You'll finish her one day.'

'I doubt it,' Matthew answered, and went on.

From the other side of the bridge he looked back, saying goodbye to a place he might not see again. The town looked very small, very humble, clustered about the cathedral, which was huge and dark against the evening sky, the central tower rising in its web of scaffolding, tier upon tier. It occurred to him then that no living man would ever see it finished, as no living man remembered seeing its foundation laid. In such a wash of time, engulfing whole generations, it did not really matter very much that one pretty girl should become a bride, her heart not in it, nor that a proud Dean should have commissioned a Mother of God that must remain incomplete. In fact, it did not matter at all.

Nothing mattered.

Matthew left the city and strayed into a labyrinth of miserable streets where the houses huddled together and clung to the city walls like unlovely and uncared-for children about the skirts of a neglectful mother. There he found accommodation in a wretched tenement where, in the cellar, bad ale was sold, very cheaply, to beggars who were lodged, even more cheaply, under the gable while, between the two, a dozen cheap-jack trades struggled for existence. It suited him to be among nameless men who would ask no questions and expect nothing of him beyond what he was willing to give—or what they might be able to steal. And not even that thought disturbed him.

Matthew, the stonecarver, must now stand aside. If I were nothing, then he was nothing too—and less. A man who looks for perfection is the greatest fool alive.

'Matthew,' I said, to the shadow at my shoulder. 'I will be a beggar, or a mountebank, or a madman—but I will not be a fool again.'

He did not answer, of course. He, poor fool, was looking at the faces and shapes of the other beggars in the room, heads like spoiled turnips, hands like knotted rope, dead faces, quenched eyes, slack jaws.

'Very well, look,' I said. 'But you will not find perfection here.'

'I envy them,' said Matthew, the shadow who was myself. 'Unlovely as they are, they are quick. Imperfect as they are, they live and breathe and perpetuate themselves.'

'Aye, they breed,' I said. 'They couple in the boozy dark and breed. While your Christs and angels smile in their stone—and do not move at all.'

A girl sat at his elbow, watching him.

'You are talking to yourself,' she said. 'Are you ill?'

Her face was pale, pinched with hunger, and she had a tooth

missing, but there was something still brave and undefeated about her. That would soon fade. At the level of famine, the stage between the child and the crone is a brief one.

'I am a divided man, not ill,' Matthew said.

The girl took his hand and turned it, palm upwards. 'Then I will tell your fortune,' she said, adding quickly, 'for a coin,' in case he misunderstood her generosity.

'I will give you a coin,' said Matthew. 'But my fortune is already spent. I shall have to go back in time, not forward, to find it.'

'It is the same thing,' she said, holding firmly to Matthew's hand which he, as firmly, closed. 'Backwards and forwards. Have you ever seen the sea?'

He had not.

'It leaves the shore,' she said. 'And goes back, far back, until there is nothing but mud and weeds, and then it returns, covering the mud and bringing fish with it. All the time, backwards and forwards.'

Matthew asked her to tell him about the sea for her penny, and to leave his fortune where it was, with the mud and weeds, but she said she could scarce remember it.

'I know only the way it comes and goes,' she said. 'And that is how it is with fortune.'

'Very well,' he said, opening his hand again. 'Then tell me that.'

But the fortune-teller's whine came into her voice and she told him no more than she thought any man would want to hear. A long journey and the overcoming of difficulties, a wish granted, a good ending. And a woman.

'No riches,' he asked, mocking her.

'No riches,' she said. 'But sufficiency. And something else, something I don't understand.'

That was more interesting. Matthew too looked at the hand she was reading and saw nothing there but what he knew already, that it was a strong hand and could have been cleaner.

'No,' she said. 'For a moment I saw something that is not possible. It must have been a trick of the light . . .'

A trick of the trade, more likely, Matthew thought. And a good one. As she peered at his hand, hesitating, his scalp tingled.

'Nothing more?'

'Nothing.'

He gave her the penny she might have had for less and went up to the sleeping-place under the gable. His shadow may have gone with him but it was lost in the darkness.

The house, like many of its tenants, had seen better days. The roof was broken in several places, and the walls oozed damp but the proportions of the room were good and it had a window which let in air. It let in the cold too and, between the cold and the effects of the sour ale he had swallowed, Matthew did not sleep well. It would be a lie to say that his thoughts kept him awake, for he had none. Apart from the cold and the discomfort of his body, it seemed to him that he had stopped existing . . .

Light comes slowly, sliding along walls and changing the shape of all it touches long before the sky begins to lose its dark. Birds ruffle their feathers and tuck their heads beneath their wings again; men stir in their sleep and huddle closer into their rags. Every dawn is heralded by a false dawn. Matthew was not deceived by it, but the room stank and he went to the window to draw a cleaner breath. His hands shook and his eyes were hot and dry as though there were stonegrit beneath the lids. He thought he must be the only creature awake in the whole city—apart from the fleas—but he was wrong.

Two people were walking in the street below—a woman whose face was hidden by her hood, and a tall, hunchbacked man in a trailing cloak. Matthew could hear their voices plainly, but not the words they spoke. He watched them idly, feeling companionship with them for no other reason than that they and he were awake in a world that slept. It was like a thread binding them. Then the woman went on toward the bridge, leaving the man alone in the street. He crossed to the opposite wall and stood, watching after her. There was something anxious and undecided in his pose; perhaps he wondered whether to follow, to wait or to go on. In the slowly strengthening light, Matthew caught a glimpse of his face, white in the grey morning, and felt the thread between them suddenly taut. Something—his pallor, a bleakness in his eyes, a general want of resolution—Matthew could not say what, but *something* in this man struck a chord he knew.

The new day was already fingering the sky, stroking the sagging roofs and edging them with pale gold while the more squalid corners were yet shrouded in what remained of night. In a nearby yard, a rooster climbed on a heap of refuse and called. Another answered him. Further down the street a door opened and a man came out, scratching his hairy belly and shaking the sleep from his head—and the hunchback, who evidently welcomed neither light nor company, whirled round and made off quickly, going away from the town.

And Matthew moved quickly too—for the hunchback's cloak had gaped as he turned, showing what was concealed beneath it. Matthew could not believe that he had seen aright but—unless he were asleep still and dreaming—this man was *winged*!

He made what haste he could but by the time he reached the stairs' foot and the arch of the street-door, the man was gone.

Part Two

Song

In au- tumn when the leaves were red, And- the ev' ning cold did sting, A hand- some lord to his la - dy sped, And she wel - comed him to her fea - ther bed where he co - vered her where he co - vered her with his wing.

Abigail T. S. Perrin

My instinct led me to the woods. What better cover could a man want than the woods that had always been my sanctuary? I had known safety among trees, learned to see, and discovered the rudiments of my craft—among trees I had thought to find myself again and be made whole. But that was yesterday, in a world where every question had one answer only. Since then, the mocking God who held my life under his own craftsman's hands had taken his chisel and, with one stroke, changed the pattern.

So I left the town behind me and followed the green road through the forest but I no longer cared for my lost youth, whether I found it again or not. It was one with my grown years, and the few good things I have made here and there, and the sense of failure that had plagued me all my life. These were the preoccupations of ghosts, tethered to their past; they were not for me, who had broken free of it. Only the winged man had any meaning now and I determined to find him again, though my entire life were spent in the search.

But it did not require a lifetime, nor even the expenditure of half a day. The path turned back on itself and turned again, ending in a grassy plot where the trees thinned out to let the light fall, unimpeded by their branches, gold rather than the green of deeper forest.

And there I found him—asleep—with the sun on his face, his breath stirring the white feathers on which his head rested, pillowed more richly than an emperor's. Always until then, whenever I had seen beauty, my hands had ached to translate it into wood or stone; to catch and preserve it for some little measure of eternity and thus, in some way, to make it my own. Yet here I felt no such urgency. This was a beauty beyond the dimension in which a maker works; it was itself outside the time that sets a limit to the life of a man or what he makes. The air trembled above him as it does above fire.

My regard must have penetrated his sleep for he sprang awake and immediately made to cover the great shining wing with his cloak. To him it was deformity—a shame to be kept hid—and nothing more.

'No!' I said, and there was real pain in my voice. 'It is beautiful! Beautiful!'

And he flinched, almost as though he had received a blow.

'A winged man,' I told him, 'is something every artist dreams of—the perfection that eludes him, waking, and that haunts his sleep. Whatever he makes can be only a hint of the perfect thing he misses . . . however he may struggle to make up the loss. Texture and grain and shape, solid and shadow . . .'

I babbled. I was afraid that, in concealing his marvellous difference, he would shrink to the proportions of any common man—and leave me bereft.

His mouth twisted.

'Beautiful, you say? But what do you know of the drag of a wing's weight, or the ache of a shoulder and breastbone not shaped to bear it? Beautiful to you—but it is not your burden.'

'The maker has a burden of his own,' I said. 'And no less heavy for being invisible.'

That made him smile, though his mouth was still awry in a way that hurt me to see.

'Shall we barter our sorrows?' he said. 'Yours for mine, mine for yours?'

'There are better ways of spending a fine morning,' I told him, and meant it. I lay back in the sweet-smelling grass and watched the clouds drift above the branches. A pair of wood warblers were busy near their nest and, in my mind, I imitated the silvery trill of their song. I was completely at peace.

'I was born with two arms like any other man,' he insisted. The wing was indeed a grief to him and this saddened me, putting a shadow on the day that had begun so well. My peace was short-lived; it flew away with the wood warblers.

I sighed. 'Tell me your story then—if it will ease you . . .'

'It is beyond belief,' he said.

I argued that most true things are beyond belief—an oak self-sown from an acorn, a butterfly wriggling from its chrysalis—we must make what we can of them.

'Then make what you can of this,' he said, and fell silent again.

I prompted him. 'You were a man like any other—'

'The youngest of eleven brothers.'

I nodded encouragement. That was a good family, one any father would be proud to own—allowing he were rich enough to keep so many alive. And here there was no hardship. The father was a great lord in his own province. His land was rich, his forests running with game. Not even his serfs counted themselves poor.

'Come now, a king,' I said. If this were a tale of enchantment, there must be princes in it.

'A great landowner,' he said. 'One who might have been a king in the old days . . .'

'And your mother was a beauty—and died young.'

'No,' he said, and frowned. 'Why do you interrupt so often? She was fair—fine-boned and gentle as a ring-dove—but not stately enough for beauty. We were happy together, as a family, but happiness is hard to define until it is lost. Certainly, she died young and then, in a while, our father married again . . .'

A new bride, jealousy and loss. It was the oldest story in the world—told first in a cave by firelight with wild beasts prowling outside, and later in a king's hall, to entertain guests after food— but now, told again in a green wood in the morning, by a man who was part of it, it was wholly new.

'And this one was very beautiful,' I said. 'And as gentle as a cuckoo.'

'More beautiful than any woman I have ever seen. And she was a witch.'

'That's in your face.'

'In my *face*?'

'An encounter with night.' I knew about the night, perhaps better than any man. I had seen its shadow come over the sun at noon and closed my eyes, shuddering. 'It's a meeting that makes us strangers to ourselves. Some become poets, others madmen. Let us say, simply, that after it you were not yourself . . .'

He laughed outright at that, but it was an ugly laugh that grated on my ears.

'Not myself!' he said, and laughter choked him. 'Why, none of us were the same. Our father, who had been a great man in all things, shrivelled to a husk of his old self. He never went out of doors again, the only world he wanted was the one small space where *she* moved. As for us, we were strangers in our own home. And Elise, our sister, no better than a drudge, to wait upon the witch and comb her hair and carry her little, shivering dog about . . .'

It was a long story—but I did not want it to end too soon for fear that, once the tale were done, the winged man might disappear on a cloud or in a lightning flash, or simply dissolve from sight as though he had never been there, in front of me, at all.

The witch had sown dissension in the family. She would say one thing to the father, another to the sons, and something else again to Elise, always twisting whatever was said in return so that it was both true and not true. It became a most unhappy house, the sons unwelcome at their father's table, and he mumbling-foolish.

'There was nothing to keep us in our father's house—yet we needed his permission to leave it.'

I understood that. An old man with a young bride might not care to have eleven handsome sons underfoot all day, but the alternative—eleven strong sons, trained in arms, at liberty in the countryside and with a sense of great wrong done—was even less to be desired.

At last the father agreed to hear their case. And that was hard, I thought, a family so divided against itself that the sons might speak to their father only in formal audience.

My winged man's voice was rough, the music gone from it. In retelling the history, he relived it and was spared nothing.

'And *she* was with him—as always. It was she who heard what we had to say, while our father nodded and dozed before the fire, scarce knowing we were in the room. He wakened from time to time but had eyes only for her. "A little wine, my dear?" he would say. "Come, drink with me, my love." And she would go to him, twine her long fingers in his hair, sip from his glass—and watch us over the rim of it.

'Yes. She listened to our grievance. Then she crossed the room and drew back the hangings from the window-space. I remember how fine and white her arm looked against the tapestry, and how dark against the sky.

'"Freedom," she said, in her purring voice. "What a high-sounding word that is on the tongues of striplings. But, very well! Be free, if that is what you want. Be free as air, my loves, be free of the whole wide heavens! *Be swans!*"

'And as she spoke, we changed . . .'

Eleven huge white swans flew from the turret window, and eleven young princes disappeared. Their father forgot them at once.

Elise went with them. She had been a drudge and now she was a beggar. She slept in barns or under the sky and, when the nights were cold, her brothers spread their wings over her—that was all they could do.

'She never lost hope,' he said. 'She always spoke as though we were men suffering an inconvenience which would pass. It would have been better for her—and better for us too—if she had given up.'

'Women will not easily give up their hope in the future,' I said. 'Without it, the race would die.'

But I thought of the girl in the winter, wandering in the cold, ragged and with her slippers worn through to the soles of her feet.

'Even when the snow came, she refused to leave us. The bushes were heavy with berries that year—and she said she was content. We were not cruel enough to drive her away.'

When he said this, I felt the pull of the warm south that must have tormented them as the days shortened. Even the most un-selfish love can be a tyranny.

'Do you credit dreams?' he asked me.

'Sometimes.'

'Elise had a dream. It told her what must be done to end our enslavement. But it was a secret, she said. She must tell no one— not even us—and for a whole year she must speak no word at all. If she failed, we would be swans for ever.'

And as though it were not bad enough to be dumb of her own choosing—when speech was all she had left in the world—she had also to gather nettles every day and tread them into flax, and spin and weave and stitch. Her brothers could not endure the sight of her patient, suffering face and her enflamed and bleeding fingers, but they were helpless. They could not speak to her and she would not speak to them. So they flew away to the marshes and came back only at night, to shelter her from the cold.

'We were ashamed,' he said. 'But if we'd stayed we might have torn her weaving apart with our beaks and trampled it with our feet. It was anger that made us callous.

'And that is how she happened to be alone when the duke came by. In the city they will tell you that her beauty struck him to the heart, that he loved from first sight—but is it possible, do you think?'

'It is always so in old tales,' I said. And I remembered the goose-girl with her golden freckles.

'A duke on horseback, a beggar-girl in a ditch? Perhaps—but only he can say what was in his mind when he spoke to her. Most likely a pert answer and a tumble in the bracken. But she gave no answer at all—d'ye see? And that's challenge enough for any man, king, duke or peasant. So he lifted her onto his horse, with all her bundles and her nettle-flax and the stalks of her day's gathering— she would not be parted from those—and carried her off to the city. It was a strange wooing—very strange—but it could not fail . . .'

'Surely,' I agreed. 'If she could not say *yes* to him, by the same token she could not say *no*. So he married her?'

Somewhere, someone had spoken to me of a duke and his dumb duchess—and I had not troubled to listen . . .

'They could have been happy together—but for her damned obstinacy. And we could have flown away and lived out our swans' lives, forgetting we had ever been men. But Elise would not break her silence and it bound us too. Months passed, the year was close to its end . . .

'Sometimes we saw our sister when she rode at her husband's side on progress from one of his houses to another. She had grown very thin. She seemed to be burning away, her eyes were huge and glittered as brightly as the jewels she wore.'

His own eyes were black and glittering. I looked from them to the feathers glowing with the reflected green of the grass and from the feathers to the long, white hand that rested on his knee. And I wondered where the man ended and the swan began.

'Was it surprising that people started to whisper of witchcraft? Was it surprising that the duke listened? Elise knew what she risked, she could have saved herself at any time.'

'At your expense,' I reminded him.

'When she was brought from prison to the stake, all the people of the city turned out in a crowd to see her burn . . . these same people who had scrambled for the coins she threw them on her wedding day, who had cried, "Long live our duchess!" and "Good health to our duchess!" As long as there's a show to be seen, men don't care much whether it's a wedding or a hanging. Not even her husband, though he was the duke and could have ordered a stay of execution with no one thinking the worse of him—not even he would raise his voice to save her. So much for human love! But *we* were her brothers, she was suffering for *our* sakes. It was our duty to do what her own husband would not, save her or die with her.'

When the executioner advanced his torch to the faggots, the eleven swans had hurled themselves from the sky to drive them back; they stood between their sister and the crowd who had come to see her burned and dared *them* to make a trial of their beaks. But none would dare.

'The guards had brought her bundles to be burned with her—a matter of common sense, but lucky. Her arms were not tied—another lucky chance. She stopped, took the bundles and, separating them, threw them to us, one to each. They were shirts she had woven from the nettles, through a year's silence and a year's pain; she had been stitching even on her way to the stake, stitching while the priest pleaded for her confession . . . there must have been agony in every stitch. When the shirt touched my own body, I cried out loud with the pain of it. Pain ran through my every sinew, every bone, every vein. But think, man, think. I had been a swan and without a voice for longer than I had any means of knowing, and now I could cry out like a man. Do you think I cared then about the pain? The enchantment was over . . .'

'And your sister free to speak of it,' I said. 'So it ended happily.'

'Happily? For some. But one of those shirts still lacked a sleeve—and that shirt was mine. And because of that lack I am as you see me now—a monstrous freak that is neither man nor bird. Do you think it ended happily for me? My ten brothers ride and hunt, they dance and make poems and pay court to ladies —they are men, but what am I?'

He rose to his feet, letting the wing spread free, each feather and pinion gleaming like snow in winter sunshine. Three times he beat the air with it—and I swear he hissed at me.

That was his story. The sun had scarcely moved at all in the telling—but it is possible to live a lifetime in the duration of a dream. And one can live a whole life's length away, and not know one is alive. An artist, a maker, straddles both worlds, I think, which gives him a freedom other men envy though it is bondage compared with the freedom he knows he can never have. Moving, as he does, in two worlds, he is at once innocent and dangerous, like an infant suckled by dragons. And, of all men, he is the most meet companion for a man with a swan's wing.

'Whatever you are, I will go with you,' I said.

Then I remembered the woman I had seen with him, when I watched from the window. It might be that the woman would not care for my company, or that she herself was sufficient company for him. So I asked about her, not wanting to join them as an unwelcome third.

And he said yes, indeed there was a girl with him. She was, at the moment, in the town getting food for the day, and would be back soon.

'She's a good girl,' he said. 'Patient, untiring and kind.'

Almost at once we heard her singing. That too was a part of her concern for him, that he should always know when it was she who came so that he would not have to hide himself as he did from others. But her concern was a natural, uncomplicated thing, she never thought of it.

I cannot say how all my senses knew that this was Gerda coming. I had seen her once, forgotten her, and found her again in stone; it was precisely right that I should see her now. And when she stooped under the low branches at the edge of the clearing and I saw that my senses had not lied, my world which had been so vast seemed to contract at once to the width of her smile. And Barney, of course, was close behind her.

She let her bunched apron drop and all her purchases tumbled out on the ground, a fresh loaf with dark hard crust, white crumbling cheese, and apples—only a little bruised, she said, and cheaper for it . . .

'You see,' said the winged man. 'This girl accepts everything

(54)

without question. Weren't you the least amazed to see a stranger with me, Gerda?'

'He's no stranger,' said Gerda, nodding across to me in a friendly way, as one gossip to another with no more than a day's parting between them.

I said, 'For a girl who can take a winged man in her stride, a stonecarver under a bush is nothing to fuss about. But I dare say Barney warned her.'

When Gerda and I had stood together by the well behind the house and watched the swans cross the sky toward the city, Barney had been very eager to see me on my way. Had he slept when this man came labouring up the slope to Gerda's goose-green, his glorious wing furled and hidden beneath the dark folds of his cloak?

'The man whom that gander approves is not yet born,' he said. 'I'm quite sure that he told her you were here. But Gerda has a will of her own, in spite of Barney, as perhaps you know.'

'*He* didn't want me to come, no more than Barney did,' said Gerda. 'But I came.'

'I shed a feather and it set her dreaming.'

Gerda would not admit that true. 'No, Lord Lothar,' she said, and turned to me again. 'It was not the feather. It was the look in his eyes more than anything. The look of someone who would rather be dead than alive—and that's a bad thing. Always.'

'When the gander saw her mind was made up, he came too. We have so much in common he sees me as a rival.'

'If you've so much in common, you should understand each other better,' she said, tartly. She hated him to jest about his wing.

'But men have much in common,' I argued. 'Yet *they* do not always understand each other.'

'They band together in common cause against anything of a different order.' Lord Lothar's bitterness was black.

'And if there is no common cause to bind them, they quarrel among themselves, like starlings over a crust.'

'Be still!' cried Gerda. 'Men quarrel—and so do birds. Do you think that geese are all alike?'

This was woman's logic. She said now what we said first—and blamed us for saying different. I loved her for it.

She divided the food between us, not forgetting Barney, and we stopped bickering in order to enjoy it. Above my head a nuthatchet clung to a branch by one leg while it supported itself by the other; the wood warblers returned, singly, and flew away again together; a chiffchaff began its endless song.

I brushed the crumbs from my hands and asked, 'What now?'

And Gerda, looking at Lothar with so much love and sadness that I found myself of the same jealous mind as Barney, told me that since every spell must have its antidote, they intended to go on together until they discovered it. She made it sound no more difficult than finding a dock-leaf to treat a nettle sting.

'But 'twould be a sad journey for a man on his own,' she said. 'And likely dangerous, with rogues about, and being . . . as he is.'

I had not thought of that, but there might well be many who would take advantage of Lothar, if they could, and turn his glory into gold and a sort of fame for themselves. He would need to be protected from such men and Gerda, who was more simple than I, had seen it at once—while I saw only the beauty and the grief.

In her childhood Gerda had been taught that every action, however small, must have a purpose before it, to keep it straight. Her own purpose never wavered. Somewhere in the world, she knew, there lived a man or woman, spey-wife or wizard, who would release Lord Lothar from the spell which bound him—and that man or woman she meant to find. She saw the end of her quest clearly on every horizon and round the last corner of every lane, but for me the quest was no more than an excuse for travelling. In Lothar I saw perfection walking, an idea at once unthinkable and profound, almost beyond imagination. It was enough, I could not care about the future, but this was hard for Gerda to understand. As she saw it, to travel without purpose was, in some way, dishonest; it invited charity by a pretence of need. And, what was even worse in her eyes, I had left my work behind without a backward thought to it, as though it did not matter. With no past to recollect with pleasure, and no future to move toward, I might as well be a common vagabond . . .

'A common vagabond,' I agreed. 'Like yourselves.'

She would not allow that they were vagabonds and denied it hotly, but it was my idleness of spirit that bothered her most.

'You call yourself a maker,' she said. 'A man who can take a chisel and mallet to a piece of stone and carve it into a tree or an angel or any shape you choose. It's a gift any decent man would want to use, not leave behind.'

'Well, what of you?' I said, with some justice. 'You were a goose-girl once, with a patch of ground to hoe, an elm tree with rooks in it, a well of sweet water, and a whole gaggle of geese for company. What are you now but a wandering girl with dust in her hair? No house, no ground, no tree, no well—and only one gander . . .'

'*I* know well enough why I left my geese on the green,' she countered. 'And so do you. But what reason had *you* to leave your work behind—beyond your own pride and the fear that your work had staled?'

'That is not a bad reason,' I said. 'Even if it were all.'

But how explain to a woman that the best and only reason a man can have for putting aside his tools *is* the fact that his work has staled, that he must gorge himself on new experience before he can work again? How explain to a girl, who has lived her whole life on one square piece of earth bounded by a hill on one side and a road on the other, that what a man makes must have his very breath in it, his heart, his pulse-beat and his mind? It needs more than his hands' skill; unless his mind sees clear he may beat his hands bloody against the stone and nothing will come of it. What can a man do then? Some go away and look and hear and touch until their minds kindle again—but that needs patience; others hold fast and copy all the things they have made before, drawing their pay and pretending, even to themselves, that their work is as good as it always was—and these I pity. Others again go mad—and I might have run wild and mindless myself but for the chance sight of Lothar. Yet how explain this to a girl who, in all her days, had seen nothing more intricate than a windflower blowing and nothing stranger than a moulted feather?

'It is more than that,' I said. 'A maker looks for perfection and never finds it. I am luckier than most . . . because Lothar is what *I* would have made, had I been able. But since he exists, and lives and walks and breathes, why should I go on looking for him in stone?'

Gerda was quiet, thinking of what I said. To be a maker was not so handsome a thing as she had supposed, nor so simple. And however I tried to explain to her what Lothar meant to me, she could not see it as true. Lothar was not perfect. He had but one arm, and a wing instead of the other, which was something to be remedied.

'You know that we journey in search of a cure,' she said at last. 'How can you bear that, when you . . . like . . . Lord Lothar better the way he is?'

I did not know how to answer her. Whatever I said, kindness and truth would be at odds, for I did not believe such a cure existed, and I could not bring myself to hurt her by saying so.

'He is without parallel,' I said, very carefully. 'But, Gerda, all things must change in time. Not even a man with a swan's wing, when he is clothed in flesh and blood, can last for ever . . .'

I was thinking of mortality. But Gerda's thoughts were centred, as always, on Lothar's recovery. She saw no other end.

'What will you do, then—when he has his arm again? Will you go back to your work?'

It was something I had not considered. But surely, if that time should ever come, which I could not believe, then there would be a change in each of us to match it.

'I don't know,' I said. 'But don't fret about it, Gerda. Let each day care for itself.'

As we went on together I had the feeling that Nature herself was not entirely happy with Lothar but skewed aside from him, behaving like a high-spirited horse trying to dislodge its rider by changing step. At first the year moved backward from June to February, where it halted a while before advancing in proper order, subdued and ready to accept what it could not change. I saw nothing odd in this. Indeed I thought it very fitting that Lothar's marvellous disorder should extend to everything about him, fashioning not only its own time but its own environment. But it worried Gerda, who lived close enough to the earth to know that such things cannot be. She said it was not so, but only my imagination running loose in my head. All the same, she was glad when the world seemed to grow accustomed to Lothar, and the year settled to a steadier rhythm with summer following spring in the familiar sequence. Then her face plumped out again and she lost the anxious look I hated to see.

It was not an easy time. Hunger became so habitual with us that after a time, it ceased to nag. True, there were days when I felt my head light and visionary, the shapes of trees and roots writhing with movement—and surely hunger was the cause. And surely it was hunger that made Gerda's hands and feet swell, and laid a shadow across Lothar's face.

Lothar grew thin. With his dark weather-greened cloak hiding his despised and glorious wing, eyes black and unfathomable in his bone-sharp face, he was a grotesque to frighten children. And not only children. If a grown man had encountered the three of us at dusk as we haunted the by-roads, with Barney like our familiar spirit, he would have turned back to the nearest church and there made such binding vows as would have kept him safe from the Devil's grip through all eternity.

As for direction, it scarcely mattered where we went, and our journey took a meandering course, following whispers and rumours rather than any known road. Between one town and the next we made long detours into lonely and desolate places to consult wise women who proved to have little more wisdom than Gerda had, and less wit. In a circle of standing stones more ancient than the moon which shone on them, we met a man who claimed he could raise the dead—for a fee—but he could do nothing to rid Lothar of his burden. Reputations for wizardry, we found, were mostly based on very mundane skills—the art of bone-setting or the concoction of herbal potions to promote desire. True enchantment, these wizards said, looking away from Lothar, was a thing of the past. One, more honest than the rest, said, 'Have done with it. Go home. Forget.'

'Forget *this*?' demanded Lothar. 'Are even wise men fools?'

Disappointments followed fast, one upon the other. The year turned slowly back, the fields and trees were bare and a March wind blew. It was the worst time of all for beggars.

We found a shallow cave, hardly more than a hollow in the hillside, but out of the wind's road. It had become our practice to gather sticks as we went along, so now I was able to light a good fire, bright enough for comfort, sparing enough to warm us till morning. Then I produced three small, withered apples from my pouch, the gift of an old crone met by the wayside, who said I put her in mind of her son.

'Supper,' I said. 'Do we roast them—or eat them raw?'

'Or save them till morning,' Gerda suggested. 'Fire and food together seems too rich for such as we. I'll wait.'

She turned back her petticoat and tore a piece from her shift, to patch Lothar's cloak for him. She cared deeply for appearances and said none of us should go in tatters until we must. That was something else she had learned from her mother, that to look poor as well as be poor was like having the Devil for a guest twice over . . . but the task grew more difficult every day, and now she was almost out of thread.

Lothar, who had been staring moodily into the fire, said, 'We could eat the gander.' I had thought of that too, more than once.

'Eat Barney?' Gerda's horror was such that I at once dismissed the thought as ignoble, though my belly gave a great, angry rumble in protest. Lothar reminded her that, even if she had not eaten them herself, she had once bred geese for the table. It was the same thing, no better and no worse. But Gerda was sure of the distinction. One could not even consider eating Barney . . .

'Why not?' said Lothar. 'He's the only plump one among us. I'd wring his neck for you, myself, if I had two hands . . .'

They faced each other. Barney, with his neck stretched forward and his wings spread, dared Lothar. And Lothar, in cruel self-mockery, craned *his* neck and let his own wing loose while, with his hand held out, he rubbed his thumb against his first two fingers, coaxingly, and made a soft, kissing noise with his mouth. Their eyes had the same shining intensity of black, and there was real malice in their jesting.

'It is not a subject for fun,' Gerda cried, throwing down Lothar's cloak and putting herself between them. Her face was white and she pressed her hand to her throat where sudden fear had set the pulse leaping.

'It was not all fun,' I said.

Barney went to his mistress at once, ashamed and sorry, but Lothar would not, perhaps could not, let the matter rest. It was absurd, he insisted, that three hungry people should travel in company with a meal that would not disgrace a king's appetite. And Barney, being a gander and therefore useless, did not even lay eggs to justify his keep.

'A gander is worth a dozen swans,' said Gerda, with spirit. 'It was a gander led the whole of Christendom in the first Holy War. The parson told me that—but I never heard of a swan doing aught for anyone . . .'

It was the first time she had spoken of Lothar's . . . difference . . . so directly, and I think it frightened her. For a moment she looked on him as a bird—to be chided, as she sometimes chided Barney—and not as a man at all.

'A dozen swans!' scoffed Lothar. 'What can a gander do save

augur the weather? And that only by means of a picked breastbone or scattered entrails.'

'I'm sorry,' said Gerda. 'I should not have said it. But all the same, Lord Lothar, Barney is my friend, and friends are not to be eaten, however hungry we be.'

It was an isolated quarrel, born of weariness and disappointment, and Gerda soon forgot it. By next morning she smiled as cheerfully as ever, and Lothar, himself contrite, complimented her on his mended cloak though he usually took her service as his due, with no need for particular thanks.

The sun shone and that made the world a better place. Gerda found snowdrops opening under a sheltered bank and, a little further on, a cluster of bright blue flowers on a creeping stem. It was called Blue-eyed Mary, Gerda said, and would soon cover the ground thereabouts with a patch of colour—if this were true spring.

True spring or not, it was a happier day. Barney disappeared for an hour and came back with a good-sized fish which it had nearly choked him to carry; I found a cabbage dropped from a carrier's cart; Lothar and Gerda sang as they walked.

Late in the afternoon we rested and ate well, toasting Barney's fish on a pointed twig and wrapping the pieces in crisp cabbage leaves to make a feast of it. No one had mentioned Lothar's wing all day or spoken of his recovery and, for once, neither had Lothar made any complaint, so when Gerda said, 'Could we not see a priest?' we looked at her, amazed.

'A priest?' said Lothar. 'Are you so anxious to be shriven?'

'Not for me,' she said. 'For you. Witchcraft and devilry overlap, I think, and priests have the power still to cast out devils. So why don't we see a priest?'

'Because, my sweet, they cannot do it,' I said, as gently as I could. 'I know priests. I was reared by one and in my profession I have met very many. None of them would I credit with the power you speak of . . .'

'No, Matthew, you're wrong. In my village there was a child who vomited pins. No, don't look like that, it's true. Her parents were ashamed and for a long time they dursn't go to church, nor anywhere. But the priest heard of it and went to them. He put his

(62)

hands on the child's head and spoke some words in a magic tongue—and, Matthew, the child was cured.'

She looked from my unbelieving face to Lothar's and back again.

'*I* believe it,' she said. 'The Devil was like a swirl of black smoke and it went out through a hole in the thatch . . .'

Lothar said, 'At least we can try. Though remembering my sister's case, I'm as likely to be burned as cured.'

And the light from the setting sun caught the tip of his unfurled wing and ran like fire along each feather's edge, staining it with crimson and gold so that his words seemed heavy with portent, and Gerda cried out, 'No. Not if you think that.'

I put my arm round her and said, 'Gerda, it is only the sun.'

The men at work in the common field straightened their backs to watch us pass, but when Gerda called out to them, 'God bless the labour!' they did not answer. Perhaps they would have been more ready to curse their labour for it brought them little good, if the prosperity of their village might be judged by its looks. It was a miserable place, hardly more than a row of hovels straddling a track that was all mud and stones. A sow lumbered across our path and a few protesting hens ran ahead of us, but we saw no other sign of life among the houses. Even the trees, for all the new green buds along their branches, had a forlorn and hopeless look, as though they doubted their own strength to bear the weight of summer. I have seldom seen a place I liked less.

Lothar said he would wait at the church so we left him there under the blank gaze of four stone evangelists sitting in a row above the beggars' bench in the porch, like so many rooks on a paling, and went on to rouse the priest from his studies—or his sleep. Barney followed us as far as the coffin-gate, then thought better of it and went back to grub among the churchyard weeds.

The priest's house was stone-built like the church, not daub-and-wattle as were the rest of the village dwellings, but otherwise there was nothing to distinguish it from them. All were equally unwelcoming, equally neglected, equally poor.

'We should not have come,' said Gerda, drawing back. 'It was the most foolish idea I have ever had.'

But I said that if we had come, we had come. There was no use in regretting it.

'Or in a month we would be saying we should have stayed. Look, the door is open. One might almost think the priest expected us . . .'

'It is because the hinge is broken,' said Gerda. 'No other reason.'

I knocked and a stray hen came clucking along the passage-way into the yard. From inside the house came the sound of some heavy object falling, and the beginning of a cry, cut short. No one came. I knocked again. Again nothing happened. But after a while, a dirty tousle-headed brat, with his shirt hiked up over his bare bum, came round the side of the house and stared at us, with his eyes very round and his thumb in his mouth. Gerda smiled at him and held out her hand, but he mistrusted her and backed away, scowling.

I knocked again, very loudly. This time we had better luck and a fat, slatternly woman came out to see who was making the din. She carried a smaller child astride her hip and there was yet another plumping her belly. She looked harassed and weary as any woman would, with a baby every year, and living in so gloomy a house, but she had been pretty once—and that not so long ago. With a little trouble taken she might be pretty again.

'Is the priest to be found here?' I asked. But at the same moment, the child on her hip began to wail and struggle. Not properly hearing my question, she answered it with another.

'Is it Sir John you want?'

'If that is the priest's name . . .'

She set down the child, which tottered a few steps toward its brother and fell. It was Gerda who picked it up and wiped the dirt from its hands. The mother had other things to worry her.

'Is it the Bishop's business again?' she demanded in a voice that was more savage than the words seemed to warrant. 'Sweet God! Will you never let the poor man be? 'Tis less than a moon ago he sent the full facts of the matter to my Lord just as was asked of him, not a detail overlooked—and what has become of Jenkyn we cannot think, for he's not back yet . . . and the cow calving . . . if the plate is gone it is gone and there's an end to it. Sir John has already told you he'll make good the loss . . .'

'It is not the Bishop's business,' I told her, when she paused for breath. 'That is his affair, but ours is no less urgent to us.'

It was a waste of words. To her, nothing was urgent except only the Bishop's business—and on that subject she seemed disposed to keep us there for ever.

'The dear man's near witless with it all,' she said. 'There's hardly a week goes by without some messenger or other from my Lord wanting to know this or that, in the very minute of his asking, not willing to wait . . . And now he threatens a visitation—though where we're to lodge him, let alone his servants, or how to feed them all, or how keep the childer out from underfoot, would fair faze God himself . . .'

I told her again, very firmly, that whatever the matter between Sir John and the Bishop, it was not our concern, and something in my voice must have convinced her for she stopped her tongue in full spate and looked at us, I think, for the first time.

'Indeed not,' she said. 'Then it will be a wedding?'

When I shook my head, she sighed deeply.

'That's a good state, marriage,' she said. 'And the duty of all Christian folk, some say.'

I was quite sorry to disappoint her, not only on my own behalf but because she sounded wistful.

'No,' I said. 'It is not a wedding. And it does not concern the Bishop. Neither does it concern any other but Sir John himself, so where may he be found?'

She directed us then, and sent her boy ahead to warn her master of our coming, but I think he strayed, as small boys will, finding something of greater interest along the road. The priest, when we found him, was not expecting us.

He was in his byre, cradling a new-born calf in his arms and soothing the cow with gentle words.

'There . . . that was none so bad, now was it, Beauty?' he was saying as we went in. 'Nothing to make so great a fuss about . . . and a fine little bull it is too . . .'

I coughed to make our presence known to him and he turned at once, his mild face still lit with tenderness, but he did not greet us until he had finished settling the little creature in clean straw. Then he rose and held out his hands.

My heart misgave me. The casting out of devils, if it can be done at all, requires a priest of a certain stamp, a fastidious mind sharpened on deep study, a high and narrow mode of life . . . I doubted if this yokel-parson would have recognized a devil if one had been shown him on a skewer.

'If it is about the Bishop's business . . .' he began. 'About the plate . . .' It seemed that no one ever came on any other errand. And then he looked at Gerda and said, 'No. It would not be that.'

His mind, like that of his woman, had started to run on weddings.

'Will you come to the house?' he offered, and looked about for the gown he had thrown aside in a corner. I picked it up for him and brushed some wisps of straw from it. God in Heaven! I thought, what a gown for a priest—threadbare, torn at hem and reeking.

He thanked me courteously and shrugged it on—but he did not come with us at once; he had still to pat the cow in affectionate farewell, praising her yet again on her morning's work . . . and to cast another glance at the calf.

'There, my Beauty! There's a brave girl . . .'

Outside in the grey daylight and the mizzling rain, Sir John cut an even sorrier figure than he had in the byre. His manner when dealing with the cow had been assured and confident but now he seemed diminished in himself, looking anxiously from me to Gerda and back again, uncertain what to do with us. Only a freak of chance could have made such a man a cure of souls instead of the capable yeoman he might have been. I hoped, devoutly, that the Bishop would abandon his plan for a visitation.

'We will go to the church,' I said. Some of his uncertainty had transferred itself to me and I thought it easier to let him see Lothar for himself than to try to explain the nature of our dilemma.

'Oh, Matthew, he is a *good* man,' Gerda whispered, as we followed him. I was quite sure of it.

Lothar sat where we had left him, in the porch. The four of us went together into the church, which was a dreadful place, stinking of damp plaster, rotting wood and the ordure of bats. Any troth plighted here, I thought, would be doomed from the exchanging of the rings onward, and I was glad now we had not come about a wedding. Silence hung, almost palpably, between us.

'Lothar,' I said, when I could stand the silence no longer. 'This is Sir John, the parish priest. I have told him nothing . . .'

I wondered how Lothar would set about presenting his case and how the priest would hear it—or indeed if the poor fellow could take it in at all. We were none of us prepared for what happened.

Lothar, without speaking, threw back his cloak—and the wing, suddenly unconfined, sprang wide, appearing to span the narrow church from one wall to the other, light leaping from every feather.

(67)

And Sir John, completely unstrung, fell on his knees, covering his eyes with the ragged, filthy sleeve of his gown.

'The Archangel Gabriel!' he moaned.

I did not know whether to laugh or rave; Gerda, I could see, was very near weeping. And Lothar, who usually wore the habit of dignity, being born to it, stood like a block, his mouth gaping. The tip of his swan's wing, his angel's wing, folded now, trailed in the musty straw.

'In God's name, priest,' I said, tugging at his sleeve. 'It's no angel—only a poor devil of a man in need of exorcism . . .'

But he was past hearing. The sight of Lothar, following so soon upon the fears and anxieties concerning the Bishop's business, had quite unhinged his mind and he was now well launched on a tide of confession that was likely to be endless. What a plague of a memory he had—and what paltry little sins. Between his fornication and the mislaying of the church plate, his conscience stung him on a thousand trivial matters. There was not an uncharitable thought nor an impatient word that he failed to bring out to air. Turn over any stone and grey things scuttle, harmless things that wither when exposed to light—Sir John made monsters of them all.

We waited. Gerda's eyes welled tears. Barney looked in through the door and watched, his head on one side. And I did nothing.

Then Lothar covered himself and it was as though the light went out of the church. Sir John's confession hiccupped to a stop and he raised his head, looking all around him with eyes that saw nothing.

'It . . . He . . . has gone,' he said, and grew calm.

'There is no one but us,' I said. 'Myself, Mistress Gerda and the Lord Lothar.'

'Then you could not have seen. The vision was for me . . .' He touched my arm with a hand that still trembled, and I lifted him to his feet. I would have continued to support him but he quietly put my arm aside.

'Truly the Lord is merciful,' he said. He went to Gerda and took both her hands in his. 'There was a radiance in this place such as the saints wrote of when the Church was young—and singing as though a thousand birds were imprisoned in the roof . . .'

He turned back to me. 'Although I have been a neglectful priest . . .' But he could not go on and fell to mumbling prayers and praises all mixed up together. Then he said aloud, 'Now I fear nothing, you understand, not even the Bishop. He who serves God can have no other master.'

We left him there, standing in the middle of his neglected church. There was nothing he could have done for Lothar, even had we been able to explain our need. And it would be cruel now to undeceive him, to rob him of his angel. He would never know such wonder again.

'Another spent day,' said Lothar. 'And nothing gained.'

But I was less sure. I had stood close enough to Sir John to hear some of what he said when his confession was done:

'I cared more for my cattle than for the people you placed in my charge . . . my children more than yours . . . saw fit to send . . .'

And, '. . . what punishment I deserved from your hands . . . yet you rewarded me . . .'

Gerda spoke what was in my mind.

'The priest gained something, I think. Perhaps it *was* an archangel he saw—and not Lord Lothar at all . . .'

It was a point schoolmen might have argued with much profit, and for many days, but metaphysics held no interest for Lothar. The priest was a fool, he was no priest, his church was sinfully kept, his flock without guidance. One could not care what such a man saw—or thought he saw.

The village was now below us in the valley, grey and unlovely under a grey sky. But clouds are never still. From a rift in the rolling mass, a beam of light shone out, briefly, to illuminate the church so that every stone in its walls stood out, distinct and separate.

'God is a jester,' I said. The thought of the priest's cow, and his fecund hearth-mate, and his boys—all weighed in the balance against one misapprehended angel—filled me with an overpowering sadness.

We were on the high downs and without shelter when night came, but Gerda slept warm under Lothar's wing.

'It is useful for something,' he said.

Neither he nor I slept. We watched the sky's varying dark and wondered about the journey, how it would end and where.

'It is too long,' said Lothar. 'Even hope must be fed or it will die.'

But my eyes were seeing a picture of Gerda's sleeping face all among Lothar's feathers—and I thought, it can never be too long.

Morning brought with it a drenching dew and Lothar rose and shook out his wing, the moisture falling from it in a fine, many-coloured spray so that, with the climbing sun behind him, he appeared to stand in the centre of a rainbow. Why could he not be satisfied with himself as he was, being so much more than a man?

All that day we followed a wide track across a ridge of the downs and saw not a single person other than ourselves. And this was strange, for it was a road made by many feet—a drove road or perhaps one used by pilgrims.

The sheep showed neither fear of us nor curiosity, as dogs would have done. Indeed, I have known dogs howl behind closed doors when Lothar passed, scenting his difference even where they could not see it—but these sheep regarded him with the same bland stare they turned on me and on Gerda, as though our being among them were of too little permanence for their eyes to register. They seemed indifferent to all merely transitory events, their minds grazing on the unknowable as their mouths grazed the sweet grass.

When evening came again we slept in a stone hut, a place such as shepherds use in early springtime when they must be near the ewes, but empty now that the lambs ran free with their mothers. Gerda lay curled on a low shelf, the shepherd's sleeping-space, which we padded for her with our cloaks. Barney tucked himself into the curve of her arm, and Lothar and I sat on the ground with our backs to the wall, our heads resting on our knees. That is a good way to sleep when travelling—only a small part of the body is in contact with cold earth—but there must be something to lean against, rock, tree or wall.

I wakened in darkness and felt that Lothar was no longer beside me. Perhaps he had but that moment quitted the hut and, in going, disturbed the air. But, to my still sleep-fogged mind, it seemed that he had been away some time. There is a sense that informs us of what happens while we sleep, and it is not often wrong. My anxiety for Lothar grew so strong that I had to curb myself from shouting to rouse Gerda and Barney to help me look for him. But there would be no sense in that. If Lothar had really gone, they would know soon enough. But if I went now, I might find him, reason with him, and bring him back.

A steady day-long wind had blown the clouds away. The moon was almost full and the landscape, bathed in a wash of light without colour, was very beautiful. I have never feared the moon, as some men do, nor thought its influence something to shut out, as did the village gossips who had peopled my childhood nights with spectres. Then the white light had soothed me—and it did so now. Furthermore, it would show me Lothar.

Not far distant a clump of trees hid a dip in the land near where the steep drop from ridge to plain was gentled by a shallower slope. I went there, and perhaps the same instinct that first led me to Lothar was at work in me—for I found him at once.

He was standing quite still, his wing raised almost to the height of his shoulder, and he was facing away from me, into the light wind. As I watched, he raised the wing yet higher—and let it drop. Raised it again, and higher yet. And down. I felt the strain as my own muscles bunched in sympathy, my shoulder ached for him.

Then he began to run—into the wind. And the wind licked his long flight-feathers and lifted him, fractionally, from the ground. Then let him fall. He turned again and pounded the air with faster and faster beats. And ran. And again the wing lifted him—and failed.

I heard him sob and saw the tears wet on his cheek as the wing dragged him round on the wind, which played with him like a cat with a mouse. And still he would not give in. Again and again he approached the wind, wooing it, and again and again it flung him down.

I was glad that the trees hid me from him. It was something he would not want anyone to see.

I crept away and sat shivering in the bothy, listening to Gerda's soft breathing . . . so warm and human in the dark . . . and trying with all my soul to forget what I had seen—Lothar attempting to fly and the very air refusing him. I wondered how many times he had left us in the night to make the same trial of his hated wing . . . or was this the first of many . . . or the first and only time? And what of Gerda? She loved Lothar with the directness and

(71)

simplicity that ruled her every action—had she ever guessed that, hidden in the depths below thought, some part of his desire was still that of a bird . . .

His difference was like the burden of royalty that cannot ever be laid aside. A king may be dethroned or imprisoned or killed—but he does not cease to be a king. Even if Lothar had met again the witch-queen who had married his father, and had she consented to unsay her spell, I think he would still have carried to his grave the shadow of a swan.

It was dawn before he returned.

Was it only the next day that we left the hills and descended to the cultivated land below? The next day or the next day after that—I cannot remember now. There were many days so alike in their weariness and lack that they could not, even then, be distinguished one from another.

There were times when we fell in with other wayfarers and shared the road for a while, but few of these encounters have stayed in my mind. Our conversation was only of the weather, or of the road itself . . .

Sitting out the noon-day heat on benches at inn-doors, we rubbed shoulders with many whose homeless condition was not far removed from our own, whose eyes glanced incuriously over Lothar's shape, seeing nothing strange. And I, in my turn regarding them, saw only their dull faces and dusty limbs, yet perhaps each carried with him a secret as inconceivable as Lothar's—some monstrous derangement of the skull, horns curled close beneath the pilgrim's wide-brimmed hat, or cloven hooves well-hid in mud-caked leather. If a man's body is but the disguise his soul puts on, what of the forms assumed by men becoming beasts or angels?

Some knowledge is buried deep—knowledge from which imagination, the soul, recoils in terror.

There were nights when I wakened, shuddering, to the sound of a voice I did not recognize as my own, crying out, 'Who are you? who are you?' and was made easy again by the sight of Lothar's human face.

Morning and noontide and night. Sunrise and zenith and setting.

Once we sat with our feet dangling in a stream while Barney caught fish for us, snapping them up in his golden beak, keeping each fourth one as his own share. Gerda wove baskets of rushes, lining them with sheep's-wool gathered from brambles, and I whittled wooden babies to lie in them—farings to sell for whatever they would fetch . . . And another day we crouched together on a

(73)

wide, empty moor while thunder crashed overhead and lightning struck at the earth all around us, blasting the one brave, wind-stunted tree to be found in all that space . . . And again we ran together down a steep, stony combe, laughing, our mouths stained with the juice of wild berries. Tiny blue butterflies flickered in and out of the feathery grasses along the path, and a patterned snake hissed at us before gliding away in the bracken . . .

And one day we came to the sea, tasting its salt on our lips long before we saw it.

'Why, how loud it is!' cried Gerda, dismayed, but Lothar smiled. He had seen it before, he said—and flown over it too.

I watched the great grey waves hurl themselves against the cliff, break in lace foam, draw back, reshape themselves and rush again, roaring, at the rocks which seemed to shudder at each impact—while gulls rode the wave-crests as fearlessly as ducks paddling in a mill-pond.

And while I watched, I heard God chuckle in my ear and say, 'Well, Matthew, can you make the sea—in stone?'

So I turned away. God knew I had left all that behind, with my chisels and my reputation. But I was troubled, being reminded of what I had thought so well forgotten. And I did not want to look any more at God's restless sea, that told me what I did not want to hear.

We left the sea and went inland again. I felt safer there, though long outcrops of rock showed through the heather like the bones of a starved beast. And we too might have starved, but for the wild bees, whose honey we stole.

'I think this is King Arthur's country,' said Lothar. 'Now, if we could find the place where Merlin sleeps . . .'

'And if we could wake him . . .' said Gerda.

'A magician easily fooled by a green girl,' I said. 'Surely we've seen magicians enough by now . . .'

'And enchantment is a thing of the past,' quoted Lothar. He was merry that day, flirting his feathers along the wind, and laughing.

No, Lothar, I thought. Not quite. *You* are the last enchantment and, but for Gerda, I would choose to have you stay as you are until death ends it . . .

That same night Death came to me in a dream and rattled his

bony fingers in my face, whispering, 'Matthew, *you* will die—but will Lothar?'

I started broad awake, but the dream stayed with me, a torment for many days. I thought of Lothar, encumbered with immortality, striding down the centuries like the wandering Jew, the man who spat at Christ as he passed with his cross, and must tarry till Christ comes again. But Lothar had also the burden of his wing and perhaps, for him, Christ's coming would make no difference.

Now it became as important to me as it was to him, that he should have his arm again. But I was sickened by the quest for wizards . . .

'Better to find your step-mother,' I said. 'And make *her* wind back the spell . . .' Though, truly, I did not see how we might manage it.

'Is that wise?' said Lothar, and shuddered. He still feared her greatly and, to be honest, so did I.

'It's a risk we must take,' I said. Gerda said nothing at all, but I know she agreed with me.

So, after a long journey, we came to his father's house—and it was empty, with thistles growing close to the door and a barn owl raising her family in the great bedchamber.

I made enquiry at the village and was told it was an unlucky place, no one went there now. They showed me a tomb in the church where a grim old warrior lay stretched out in stone, his gloved hands folded on the hilt of his sword, and his feet resting on a swan. That was the old lord, they said. I asked about his wife, his *second* wife, but they knew nothing of her. The only wife they knew had been a sweet lady, often ailing, and dead long since.

'And what became of his sons?' I asked.

'Oh, aye,' they said. 'His sons.' Which was no answer.

I returned to the house, where I had left Lothar and Gerda, and the three of us went together from room to room, upstairs and downstairs, courtyard and closet. There was nothing to discover. Hangings that Lothar remembered as bright, glowing with colour, crumbled into dust when we touched them; the massive oak table in the hall had been carved and channelled by beetles till it was no more than a shell, spilling white powder when I smote it with my fist.

'An unlucky place,' I said.

We climbed a treacherous winding stair to a room in a tower, a round room with a small hearth and a wide window. Jackdaws had littered the sill with tinsel trash but the spiders had been there since and hidden it beneath layers of their grey lace.

'This is where it . . . happened,' said Lothar.

But there was nothing to see, not even the chair where his father had sat, sipping from a jewelled cup and smiling into the eyes of his witch-wife.

'There should, at least, be ghosts . . .' Lothar said, and Gerda whispered, 'I think *we* are the ghosts.'

'I should have asked at the village,' I said, trying to keep my voice light. 'They might have told me that these rooms are haunted by two men, a girl and a goose . . .'

The hair rose at the back of my neck and I felt drops of sweat, like ice, along my spine.

'Come away,' said Gerda. 'Come away.'

'There must be something,' Lothar argued. 'I spent my boyhood here. Is there no toy of mine, no child-sized arrows, no cup or platter to speak out and say I lived, however long ago?'

'Did you never hide treasure in the boards?' I asked, thinking this something any child might do. I had hidden my own treasures, my wooden beasts and birds, all about the forest.

'Never,' said Lothar. 'There was always so much. Why value one thing higher than another?'

'It would all be used, not kept,' said Gerda. 'But come away.'

'A buckle,' I said. 'A bridle-strap? Something not valuable in itself but kept because of an association, a memory . . .'

'There was always tomorrow,' said Lothar. 'We had no need of memory.'

'Come away,' said Gerda, again.

I looked through the window-space, where the ivy was already creeping in.

'You never see it move,' I said, pulling at a tough stem. 'Yet it is always at work, dislodging stones and binding them together . . .'

'You never see time move,' said Lothar. 'But you know when it has passed.'

Framed in ivy, the landscape looked very peaceful, very calm, unpeopled. A small lake, scummed with green, reflected nothing; the sky was empty of birds . . .

'That's odd,' I said.

'Why,' said Lothar. 'It is all odd. What one thing more than another?'

Because of Gerda's fear, I would not say. But on coming into the room I had glanced through the window, quickly, not much concerned, and surely I had seen an acreage or so of corn, bending under its own golden weight. Now there was nothing but black stubble . . . It struck me as more portentous, more sinister, than when, earlier in the year, the seasons had turned widdershins in response to Lothar's most unnatural presence. That I could understand. But this was his own world. There was nothing natural here to be affronted by his aberrant form. It was Gerda and myself who were out of place . . .

I looked at Gerda and saw little crow's-foot lines springing from the corners of her eyes, a hardly discernible slackening of the flesh beneath her jaw—but I could not remember if these signs had been there yesterday, or even an hour before, though Gerda's face was more familiar to me than my own. Then I looked at Lothar, seeking the same marks of age—and there were none. Lothar's face was smooth.

'Nothing,' I said. 'No, there is nothing here.'

And I turned my back to the window, afraid that another moment would show the lake iced over and snow falling.

We left the house and its lands behind us and found the road again, a solid, sensible road with wheel-ruts in it, and sharp stones, and tall hedges on either side. We crossed a ford, with the water rising almost to our waists, and dried ourselves in the late sun, lying in a churchyard with a round wall.

It was a small church—a dozen souls would have been cramped in it—but the porch was very fine, intricately carved with dragons and serpents all enlaced, each caught and struggling in what seemed to be the coils of another but which proved, when I traced the pattern through, to be its own writhing tail furnished with a second head. The low arch of the door was supported by columns of bearded men, each standing firm on the head of the one beneath, and frowning fiercely at the weight of the one above. Good work and old—made by a man who knew how to laugh. I walked round the church to see what heads masked the water-spouts, and these also were good—rams, bulls, owls and eagles—no two the same.

But there was something else—something I liked less well. On the blank north wall, facing away toward the trees which came close on this side, was a crude carving in low relief—a squatting woman, her most secret parts displayed, and her grinning face an invitation to lewdness. I had seen her sort before and knew what she was. We called her the witch-i'-the-wall, and country women touched her when they wished to be with child, though the Church frowned on the practice. I had never given her much thought except to wonder why the Church let her stay—old heathen thing that she was. But this one I hated. She seemed to be compounded of many evils and her lewdness was only a fragment of what she was. I felt her draw me to her and this was worst of all. If the Devil had sired me, then this ugly mockery of woman was my dam.

And she spoke to me in my head:

'Eh, Matt, luv, what a fine girt plowman thee'd been, surely, left t'theeself, afore th'Owd Man took 'ee. And look at now what bist about, ploddin' behind summat 'ee might've dreamed. Wi' a wench too—tumble 'er, Matt, tumble 'er and ha' done.'

There was more besides, words and images mixed, all warm, dark, cloying. The voice was heavy and chuckling, rich as loam, but there was something wrong with it, as though the tongue were too big for the mouth that contained it, as though the creature had not been made for speech at all.

No, whatever she had been made for, it was not for speech. It was *my* mind she was using and *my* tongue and *my* words. Perhaps my feelings too—but all twisted to her own needs, which were dark and groping . . .

'What be wrong then, Matt? Don't 'ee want 'er?'

Ah, yes, I wanted Gerda, had wanted her when I first saw her on the green, had wanted her ever since. But Gerda loved Lothar. And so did I.

'Did th'Owd Man castrate 'ee, Matt? And give 'ee a carvin' tool i' place o' what 'e took? But don't 'ee fear, I'll put 'ee right again . . .'

Round the corner, Gerda lay in the long grass, with her eyes closed, waiting. And what sort of a rival was Lothar? A swan can deal a heavy blow with his wing, I thought, but he's no match for a man . . .

The witch might have won me—had she stopped at that. But she went further.

'. . . a girt man to be playin' wi' a bit o' stone . . .' she said.

And again, '. . . stone won't keep 'ee warm, Matt.'

She over-reached herself and was defeated, belittling stone to me, for stone had been my first love, which is the love a man never forgets. My mind hardened against her and I said, aloud, 'And what are you, old witch, but a bit of stone, not even well cut?'

She shrank back into the wall, silent. A piece of ugliness left over from the past, something best forgotten. And I turned the corner of the church, into the sunlight.

'Well, Matthew, what did you see?' asked Gerda, sitting up and stretching her honey-golden arms.

'Birds and bulls,' I said. 'And a witch with sharp knees and one eye bigger than the other . . .'

We got bread at the priest's house and I told him I liked his church. He sighed and said, 'It's well enough, but too old. I doubt it was built by Christian men at all.'

The year dropped toward autumn but the heat stayed oppressive, a blanket smothering the fields, night and day. Lothar suffered exceedingly beneath the weight of his long cloak and Gerda was exhausted. Her shoes had quite worn away and her feet were bruised, often bleeding. We all endured much from flies.

I said, 'When we come to a town, we will stop. For the winter, if need be.' But Gerda said a little rest would do, she needed only a little rest and, for Lothar's sake, we must not stay too long.

I reminded her that we must replenish our common purse before going on. While she rested, I would work and with luck we need not beg again until the following spring. But she replied that the purse had something in it still. It would be better to travel while the weather held good.

Our progress was very slow and seven dragging days went by before we came within sight of a town. The trees were now more gold than green but the leaves did not fall, there was no breeze to take them. And still the heat continued. The last day seemed hardest of all, and it was deep dusk when we reached the first of the houses. Deep dusk and not a light showing. I knocked at several doors, hoping to buy bread, but got no answer. Then, thinking it foolish to starve amid plenty, I clambered over a wall and stole vegetables for our supper, expecting at every moment to be seized by the householder or to feel his dog's teeth in my leg. But no one came.

The lanes were deserted too, and so was the church crypt where we had thought to spend the night. Even the church was in darkness except for the lamp on the altar and one candle, almost spent, before an image of Saint Sebastian shot through with arrows. That should have warned me—but hunger and weariness clog the mind so that it often fails where it should be most alert.

A crypt is a cheerless place when there is no company of beggars to enliven it, but it was cool after the stifling streets. I left Gerda there, with Lothar and Barney to guard her—and the stub of a candle, taken from Saint Sebastian without his leave, to light them—while I went into the open again to fetch water from the public conduit.

The entire town was dark, every house shuttered, every door bolted—yet it was not wholly deserted. Some of the tenements I passed were clearly habited, with sounds of merriment coming from behind the shutters—but it seemed to be a mournful sort of revelry, ale-songs intermixed with dirges, and wails with laughter, in a manner that struck me as singularly unpleasant . . . even before I knew the cause. And once I stumbled over a body which groaned and cursed me. Supposing the fellow to be drunk, I hefted him into a passage-way between two gaunt buildings, where he might lie safe from robbers—if he had not been robbed already—and went on. When I fell upon a second body—one that did not groan—my mind started to work again.

Saint Sebastian, I remembered, protects the devout from plague. The candle lit to him, the shuttered houses and empty streets—all told the same tale—but I had to fall over a corpse in the dark before I understood. There was pestilence in this town. Had we approached by the King's road, no doubt we would have met people fleeing, all their portable goods in carts and bundles; we would have heard their news and turned aside from the place. But we used the highway only when we must, and news travels slowly or not at all along the tracks we followed. We had met no one. No use to think of that. We were here—and so was the plague.

So what to do? Make away—or brave it out?

We had no choice. Gerda could not go further, I was sure . . .

But if, for that reason, we *had* to stay, why then, we could turn the sickness to our own advantage. With many houses abandoned and the others shuttered and barred, we might forage as we liked in the neglected gardens . . . whatever happened, whatever risk we took, we would not go hungry. Lothar and Barney together would keep intruders from the crypt, and I would provision it to withstand a siege. We would not only rest—but grow fat. And, being at leisure, I would make new shoes for Gerda. Surely I should thank God for the pestilence.

I walked on, treading warily, and even laughing a little to myself.

But there was another corpse in the market place, sprawled out beneath a partly dismantled booth. I stopped laughing and crossed myself instead. And there was another, fallen across the mouth of the water-pipe . . . which meant I would have to look for a cleaner source, if we were not to perish too. So I crossed the square again and turned up another street, wishing I had a lantern, any light other than the stars to guide me . . .

And, as sometimes happens, even as I wished it, my need was answered. I saw a light ahead of me at end of the street—a somewhat wavering light, pausing and moving on. I followed. The man who carried it was holding it sometimes high, the better to peer in doorways at either side, and again low, as he crouched over—and fumbled—the dreadful things he found. A scavenger, I thought, a robber of corpses—and the bile rose sour in my throat. Well, I would have his lantern. Let him go about his dark trade in the dark.

It should have been a simple matter to wrest it from him—but he moved quickly and used my own strength against me so that I fell full-length on the ground, hoping he would not be as quick with his dagger. Yet he did not close with me . . .

Standing back and surveying me quite coolly, he said, 'Well?'

One word, not what I had expected, and unanswerable.

'Well,' I said, echoing him. I sat up and got my breath again. 'That was a neat trick for a corpse-robber . . .'

'A corpse-robber?' he said. 'Why, man, I am a physician. But what are you?'

I told him I was newly come to the town and in search of water.

'It was your lantern I wanted, not your life,' I said, and he told me that if I dared to go with him, he could let me have water, clean and sweet, from a well at the back of his house.

He had a hand-cart nearby and had been engaged on his nightly foray through the town in search of the afflicted, those whom he might still help with his medicines. He was not a robber but a deliverer.

'An understandable mistake,' he said, and bore me no ill will for my rough attack on him. By the time his house was reached, we were quite companionable.

It is strange that, though I knew his trade, I was so ill-prepared for the stark evidence of it. There are times when the mind sleeps, or shows only the pictures one would choose to see and, while I listened to the physician, whose name was Corvinus—a good name for a scavenger—speaking of his travels in Spain and Arabia in quest of medical knowledge, my mind had shown me a plain, comfortable room with books, a room where one might sit and listen, learning much about the world . . . Certainly, I do not grow wiser with age.

The room I entered, following Master Corvinus, was not like that at all.

In every available space a makeshift bed had been set up; each bed was occupied and every occupant bore, unmistakably, one or another of the hideous signs of his affliction. A fire burned in the centre of the room and clouds of sulphurous smoke hung in the air, the stench both warring and combining with the stench of sickness and putrefaction.

'Now,' said the physician, his voice harsh. 'Do you fear the plague?'

Fear is one of the prime movers in the lives of men. The crusading knight, I suspect, is pricked on less by his love of God than by his fear of damnation; the monk buries himself in the cloister as an escape from war or women—or both; a hero is only a coward with his cloak turned the other way. Every man has his own secret fear, the one he cannot explain but which goes as close with him as does his guardian angel—but there are great fears beside, that are common to all men. The fear of pestilence is one of these.

'Any man who says he does not fear the plague is a liar,' I said.

Corvinus set down his lantern and the shadows shrank.

'Then you had better go,' he said. 'Every breath exhaled between these walls is tainted, the scourge respects no one. Even the priest who came three days ago to shrive the dying, is himself dead. This morning I dragged his corpse into the yard. And there it waits, with the others already lying there, until I am free to bury them. I will show you the well—you need not fear that, I keep it covered against pollution—and I will give you a lantern . . .'

'Not so fast,' I said. 'I fear the plague as much as any man does—but we must all die of something, sooner or later. The pestilence is just one agent among many.'

For a minute or so, he did not answer, seeming to weigh my words for their truth. During this time I observed his face, noticing that he was blind in one eye, the left, which was shrivelled and half-hidden by a drooping lid. That side of his face too was seamed by an old scar, and his mouth twitched up at the left corner which gave him, from one angle, a certain goblin look. He was a man with two separate faces and I thought he watched me with both.

'And that's a boastful speech,' he said, at last.

'I did not mean it so,' I said. 'But come, I will strike a bargain with you. I will stay and bury your dead—and in return . . .'

'Yes?'

'You have told me something of your life. Would it be true to say you have encountered, and perhaps studied . . . treated . . . cured . . . diseases not in the general common run?'

'Yes. That would be true.'

'Malformations? Abnormalities of the human frame?'

'Those too.'

'The fact is this,' I said, hardly knowing how much I dared to say. 'I travel with a friend who suffers a peculiar malady—a malformation of the shoulder and arm. I will bury the dead and help you, as far as I am able, with those who live. And, in return, you will try your skill on my friend. That is fair.'

'More than fair,' said Corvinus. 'You take a great risk for your friend. But I need your strength. While the dead remain long unburied, the pestilence spreads without hindrance. Together, we may contain it. So I will throw something else in the scales—to lessen my debt to you and make your risk more worth the taking. I have a small house outside the town, with its own vegetable patch, an orchard and a deep well—a goat too, if no one has stolen it. Let your friend wait there until we are through, and then I will treat his arm.'

'If we are still alive,' I said, and our bargain was struck.

Corvinus, a very trusting crow, gave me the key of his house, and a leather flask of water for my friends' immediate use. I thanked him and made my way back to the crypt, where Gerda was beginning to fear that some harm had befallen me. Lothar smiled wryly when he heard my plan.

'A physician? to *this*?' he said, shaking out his feathers. In that

(84)

setting he looked like a broken stone angel stowed away in a vault to await repair.

But Gerda clapped her hands together and cried, 'Why not? We've tried wizards and wise women to no purpose. And we've tried a priest. We never considered a physician—but why not?'

'A wing is very like an arm,' I said, remembering anatomical sketches I had made during my apprenticeship. 'And this man is skilled . . .'

The next morning I left them at Corvinus' country place. Neither the goat nor her kid had been stolen, and the garden was as well stocked with herbs as it was with cabbages. The apples were ripe and ready to drop, and in the yard a few noisy hens were cooped up, clamouring for release. I envied Gerda and Lothar their ease and luxury and went, most reluctantly, back to my bond.

That day I shovelled earth until I thought my back would break, tumbling corpses all uncoffined into a common grave to let the earth work on their corruption. It was a good labour. Death cuts us down to one size—merchant and peasant, fair and hideous alike— there is no distinction. And neither is there a distinction between those awaiting burial and those who bury them . . . which is stranger. Many years before, a dead badger had taught me to use my eyes; now a dead priest taught me—as no live priest could— that death is the shared inheritance of everything that breathes. I said a prayer for the priest as I covered his staring eyes with earth. God knows there are priests who flee from the pestilence as from the Devil, and send letters of consolation to their flocks from a safe place, reminding them that in such perilous times each man may shrive his neighbour and God will save them all. The priest I buried had not been of that kind, he did his duty and God served him death. It is something I shall never understand.

At first I wondered about the lives of those I interred with such scant ceremony and my speculations were, in sort, a mourning—as when the kin of a dead man gather together and regale each other with tales of his doings in life, giving him a brief extension of mortality. But before long I had ceased to think about such matters, and the corpses I tipped from the physician's cart were so much carrion, the breeding place of worms, no more.

Between us, Corvinus and I brought many in from the streets

and lanes—the living to lie in the places newly vacated by the dead, and the dead to lie in the graves I dug for them. Some I buried at night, by the light of a lantern. The red and saffron gleam threw into prominence the angular contortions of their limbs; the tension of a spine arched in intolerable pain; a grin that here bared teeth to the very roots . . . or there, in a corpse where the first stiffness was relaxing into calm, melted into a smile that was almost one of peace. A lantern's flame gives an inconstant light and, playing upon the pit, gave to its contents an illusion of movement—which brought my thoughts round to stone again, for movement has always led me back to stone, as stone has always vexed me by being still. I leaned on my spade and thought how I might combine these shapes in a sculptured frieze that would remind the living, not of Hell—which is a concept my heart rejects—but of mortality.

When our work was done and our charges made as comfortable as might be, we would sit together in a room upstairs, where a fire of sweet-smelling wood—ash, juniper and laurel—burned in a brazier near the door, the smoke making a curtain between us and those who lay below.

'The end is always the same,' I said. 'They die here—or in the streets. Does it matter where?'

Corvinus, who had been sitting, elbows on table, the scarred side of his face hidden by one hand, looked sharply at me.

'It does matter,' he said. 'Are you thinking, perhaps, that the dead are not able to pay for their care?'

Indeed, that had occurred to me but the thought, once spoken, sounded uglier than I meant.

'Only that you tend them, they die, and I bury them,' I said. 'I bury them, wherever they die, and it makes a difference neither to them nor to me. Yet does it not dishearten you, who are a physician and therefore looking toward a cure?'

'There is no cure for the pestilence,' he said, putting his head in his hands again. 'It runs its course . . . and I think it burns itself out or becomes sated by what it feeds on. After it has raged a while, it takes fewer victims and, of those, many recover. Always the same pattern.'

Pattern was something I understood.

'By studying the pattern,' I suggested, 'you may find a cure.'

'One may prevent, I think,' he said. 'I doubt if one may cure . . .'

Yet it seemed he was not without hope. There were times when he bled the afflicted, though with a restraint that was rare in one of his calling.

'If the disease attacks the heart,' he explained, 'we may be able to draw it away by means of an incision in the arm-pit; if the liver lies under siege, we make our incision at the groin. But this leads to a cure only when the epidemic is almost spent—at any other time it may do no more than add suffering to suffering. If a man must die, let him die with dignity . . .'

And so they did. He gave them soothing drink—mixtures of apple-syrup, lemon, rose-water and peppermint; he heard their last confessions with proper solemnity, prayed with them and held their hands in his own to ease the last awful spasms that meant death. And he never let the dead remain with those who lived, for a moment longer than was necessary. The corpse removed, the straw was taken out and burned, the floor fresh-scrubbed and powder of sulphur and antimony thrown on the fire. Each night another victim, brought in from the street where he had been abandoned by his kin, was laid down on new straw.

'How long?' I asked, harking back to the pattern.

'A few months,' he said. 'Not longer. But much depends on the weather—heat feeds it, cold clamps it down . . .'

A few months, I thought. Perhaps by Christmastide Lothar would have his arm again. He would marry Gerda and, for me, the world would be a poorer place—but that was something I had schooled myself to face. By Christmastide, Lothar would have his arm . . .

I had great faith in Corvinus, he was a practical man after my own heart. He had been imprisoned once for throwing a priest, bodily, out of a sick-chamber—and I admired him greatly for that . . .

'Which is not to say I stand against the Church,' he said. 'But let the priest come in later, when the physician can do no more. Before that point is reached he had better stay outside and chant his prayers at a distance. I have never seen the virtue in saving a man's soul at the expense of his flesh.'

'I wish it were as easy to throw a priest out of a mason's yard,' I said.

And then I asked him about his scar, thinking he might have got it in the foreign wars. He had spent some time with the army, I knew.

'No,' he replied. 'I got that from a madman. His kin supposed him possessed, and took him to a priest for exorcism—which, to the madman's logic, was a sort of insult. He knew perfectly well why he wanted to kill his wife—the devils were in *her*, he claimed, and his knife would let them out more surely than would any priest's hands on her head . . . If the priest prevented him, why then, the priest must also be possessed. So he let his wife go and attacked the priest instead.'

'And you chanced by and saved the priest?'

'I was the priest,' he said. 'And I think that madman's knife let a little sense into my skull. When I recovered I turned to medicine and, because the Church decrees that men vowed to religion should not touch those things which cannot honourably be mentioned in speech—and here I quote you from a Church council— I had also to turn my back on the Church . . .'

I looked again at the man's two faces and marvelled at the economy that had set them together, side by side in one flesh, in a way that no carver, working in stone, would have dared—and I saw their meaning now.

'The plague has returned you to your first office,' I said. 'This morning you gave absolution to two men, and they died in a state of grace.'

He shrugged. 'Had you performed the rite, it would have been the same. The pestilence makes priests of us all.'

Yes, that I knew. But, none the less, I had seen some special hallowing in the physician's priestly ministry that mine would have lacked.

'Does the Church divide Christ?' I asked. 'Do these noble churchmen, who pass decrees in council, distinguish between Christ the healer, and Christ the son of God?'

'Hush!' said Corvinus, laying a finger on his crooked mouth. 'Christ was not a surgeon; he did not let blood.'

So the plague ran its riot through. The toll of the dead diminished, the last victims rallied and recovered, and slowly the town returned to its normal daily round. It was good to see men walking in the streets again, and to hear the church-bells ring. And it was good to see the living decently mourn their dead, the wives and brothers and aunts and cousins they had put out of doors to die . . . or be cured . . . according to God's will, as they saw it, or God's whim. They were a little troubled at first by my unlicensed graveyard, but that was soon put right by an anxious-looking fellow sent by the Bishop to consecrate the ground that our dead profaned, and to say a Mass for their souls. And to praise God that the pestilence was over.

Corvinus threw open the shutters of his house, and together we scrubbed it clean from attic to cellar, strewing herbs on the boards and flagstones in every room. Then he said, 'Your side of the bargain is done. Now fetch your friend here.'

For the first time since I had met the physician, I began to doubt. Though I had seen his skill and knowledge manifested in more than a dozen ways, though I knew his patience with the suffering and his anger at their sickness, though I trusted him as I trusted Gerda—now that the time had come, I doubted if he or any other man could help Lothar.

I whispered as much to Gerda, sorry beforehand for her disappointment. But she squeezed my hands and whispered back that all I had risked would be counted nothing if we did not try. And Corvinus was waiting.

Gerda and I sat together on a bench while Lothar, trembling a little, folded back his cloak and offered his marvellous plumage to the physician's examination. I had been curious to see how this very practical man would receive so incredible a supplicant for healing—would he regard my friend as a human soul in need of succour . . . or as a bird? Or would his priest's mind expand to encompass the possibility that I had brought an angel to him? I watched.

Perhaps one needs to be a visionary, a madman or a saint to see strangeness even where strangeness is—and Master Corvinus was none of these. He laid his hand on Lothar's wing as though he saw such every day.

'I see nothing seriously wrong,' he murmured. 'These *remeges*, the large flight feathers . . . primary, secondary and scapular . . . are as they should be . . .'

His fingers probed, lifting and smoothing each feather as he spoke.

'The quill shaft, you understand, has a hollow basal part, the *calamus*, embedded in the *dermis* or inner layer of the skin, and also a solid distal part, the *rachis*, supporting the vanes . . . Truly, a wing is a splendid piece of work . . .'

Lothar scowled. 'Nevertheless,' he said, his voice tight with irritation, 'nevertheless, it is a wing!'

Corvinus raised his head and looked directly at him. 'And there is nothing amiss with it. It is structurally sound. So why have you come to me?'

'The feathers,' said Lothar, gritting his teeth. 'The feathers, man! The wing itself! Is it not clear enough to you?'

I felt for him. Yet can a man be cured of what is not diseased? The physician, in his way, was right.

'There is no blemish in your plumage, Lord Lothar,' he said. 'No fractured pinion, no unseasonable moult . . .'

'But I am a man,' Lothar insisted. 'Excellent as this wing may be, I would liefer be without it. You are a physician and surgeon, Matthew tells me, can you not take your knife and cut me free of it?'

I had not thought of that solution and neither had he, I am sure, until he spoke. It was simple and obvious—but my mind flinched from it.

I might have trusted Corvinus better. He lived according to a standard the world has almost forgotten.

'I am a surgeon,' he said. 'Not a butcher. I have never, in all my life, cut into flesh that was clean and healthy. Even had I found inflammation at the *calamus*, proof of some infection, I would have given you a salve for it rather than use my knife. But there is no infection . . .'

'Which means you can do nothing,' I said.

'There is nothing to be done,' said Corvinus.

'You must admit the inconvenience,' I said. 'A wing is not an easy appendage to carry through life.'

'I grant you. But life is not an easy thing. I have seen men so

(90)

distorted in their frames that every unconsidered movement caused them agony. Great pain, Lord Lothar, not inconvenience. And I have seen cheerful lepers, hobbling on their stumps, thanking God for his present mercies, and not enquiring too closely into the future. You must learn to live with your wing, Lord Lothar—as you, Matthew, must learn to live with God.'

I let that pass, being in no mood for theological argument.

Lothar said, 'I cannot live with it . . .'

And Corvinus sighed, very deeply. 'Cannot is a hard word,' he said. 'And mostly meaningless. If we must, we can—and here I see no alternative. I will give you an ointment for your shoulder muscles, which are somewhat tense, and wish you a good end to your journey. Matthew, I am still in your debt.'

'Not so,' I said. 'You have housed and fed us. Gerda has rested well and we are no worse off than we were before.'

Yet that was not quite true. For Lothar this was another failure to add to all the rest—and winter was approaching.

We could have wintered there. Corvinus offered us his house to use as our own, but there was nothing to be gained by staying . . . now that we were rested, fed and well shod again. We even had a full purse between us, the gift of a grateful tradesman whose son had recovered from the sickness. Corvinus should have had that money, not I, but he said he had no need of it and I did not argue.

Lothar was steeped in gloom. He trudged beside us in silence, dragging his wing so that some of the feathers at its tip were spoiled. This angered me.

'You should do as Corvinus said,' I told him. 'Learn to live with it. They say a blind harpist plays the sweetest music—and perhaps there is compensation in a wing too, if you but give yourself the chance to find it . . .'

Words. The language a man uses to hide his thoughts from other men. I neither believed in a remedy as Gerda did, nor longed for it as did Lothar. The feathers that had shone, rainbow-hued, in the warm rain of springtime, now glittered like frost under the red winter sun. And he dared to muddy them.

It made Barney angry too. His own grooming was thorough and constant. I think the old goose who hatched him from his egg must have been like Gerda's mother in her ideas of what was right and proper.

'Barney,' I said. 'You have two good serviceable wings—and you are rightly proud of them. Lothar has one and it is useless—yet his thrills my very soul and yours do not. Why is this, I wonder?'

Lothar thought I mocked him, but indeed nothing was further from my intention. Whenever I looked at him now, I felt my hands awaken. And my mind, that had once always stirred with my hands, began to awaken too and told me that, with two wings, Lothar might have seemed an angel—a concept envisaged by many and therefore knowable. With his single wing, set on a man's shoulder and balanced on the other side by a human arm, he broke the pattern, making something new. There is a hesitation before each chisel-stroke, a moment of decision so brief as to pass unnoticed. If this hesitation could be given form, that form would be Lothar, or something like him.

'Oh, be content,' I said.

We might have quarrelled but, at that moment, our path turned a corner and we saw ahead of us the walls and towers of a city, very small in the distance, looking as compact, as contrived, as one depicted in a Book of Hours.

'Not there,' Gerda said at once. 'Not a city. A small town perhaps—but nothing as fine as this . . .' And this was the goose-girl who had sat on her green with her birds all round her, and longed to see the city with all the passion of a saint longing for Heaven.

'We cannot walk all winter,' Lothar said. His voice was decided, his words reasonable, so paying no attention to Gerda's pleading we left the by-way and followed instead the wide, well-kept road that wound round and down toward the city gate. It was a long road too, and sometimes seemed to lead away from the city rather than toward it but always curved back again to show the walls larger and more clear, with tiny mannikins going in and out.

'It looks . . . unreal . . .' said Gerda, but that was fancy. Nothing looks real to the one standing outside, and dreams are real enough when we are in them. Another curve of the road, a bridge with five arches and a chapel, some trees, yet another curve—and now the little figures were nearer man-sized, and the towers had windows, and there were banners flying.

'Do you like it better?'

'I like it less,' said Gerda. She would have added something in explanation, I think, and we might have listened . . . but it was then we had our first sight of the Countess Almira, and after that nothing was quite the same. The proper moment for speaking was lost.

She rode a pure white mare of the breed called Arab, a high-stepping, delicate beast with a long sensitive head and silver mane. And she herself was white, her skin lily-pale, her hair like flax braided with pearls and veiled with white gauze. Her gown was white too and her eyes, like the horse's mane and like the bells on her harness, were silver.

I have heard people say that marble is white—and so it is when the sky behind is dull or clouded but, even then, white only by contrast. More usually it glows, rosy in morning or evening light, and at midday, when the sun touches it, veined with warm gold. The Lady Almira was white to the core, white as snow lying deep, and so cold that she burned.

The lords and ladies with her were dressed in scarlet and green and gold, but their colour was colourless beside her white. We stood aside to let them pass and, when the Lady drew abreast of us, Lothar swept off his shabby hat and bowed almost to the ground. It was a showman's gesture, his vanity answering hers, and I did not care for it at all. She, on the other hand, liked it very well. Her silver glance flickered over him and she said something I did not hear to the man who rode at her side. He turned his head to stare at Lothar.

They went by—but the Lady had paused to look at Lothar and Lothar had looked at the Lady. Something ended then and something else began. Gerda knew it but she said nothing.

Men still sing of the Countess Almira, praising her beauty, courtesy and wit, and the songs will outlive her beauty to become a part of every minstrel's stock-in-trade for generations yet unborn. But in the stews and taverns of her own city, other words were sung to the melodies—and somehow I think those songs will live even longer.

At that time, however, we knew nothing of this lady. Our only concern was to find a winter lodging in her city and, more immediately, a sleeping-place for the night for, when we went through the gate, it was already evening.

Inns vary greatly in the accommodation they offer and in what they charge for their service; the best are too crowded for comfort and some others have room to spare simply because of the reputations they have earned for ill-cooked food, sour ale and infested straw. A stranger entering an unknown city at nightfall, with nothing to guide him, has little choice but to take what he finds and, if it fails to satisfy, to look elsewhere next day.

But we were fortunate. The gatekeeper directed us and we came to a well-appointed house where the trestle-tables, at which a few people already sat, were scrubbed clean of grease, and where the fire had a good draught of air to send the smoke up the chimney rather than back into the room. Also there was the smell of bread baking, which promised a good board; it was altogether a wholesome and welcoming place.

I ordered food and drink, counting the coins one by one from a small purse so that it might be seen we were not worth the trouble of robbing, then went with our host to inspect the outhouse where we had chosen to be lodged as less costly and more private than a room. This small business concluded, I returned to my friends who were sitting together in the darkest corner, Lothar with his cloak close-wrapped about him as though he were a man oppressed by cold.

We had attracted some notice, of course. Wayfarers are usually worth a second look—the first being to assess their wealth, the second their honesty—and perhaps a third, to search out a good tale. In any case we were not quite of the common run—two men, one a hunchback, the other as ugly as a Barbary ape, in company with a girl and a fine gander. The men at the tables stopped their conversation to look at us, and I nodded back at them, friendly but not too eager.

The room filled and, in a little while, we were joined by another guest, not a townsman but an itinerant pedlar, a purveyor of pins and knacks, trivial things such as lonely women buy more for the sake of the gossip given away with them than for the goods themselves.

Sitting down, he introduced himself: Abel Oake, at our bidding. I grunted, Gerda nodded and Lothar gloomed at him across the table. He refused to be discouraged.

'Have you come far?' he asked, and I saw his mind storing away the reply even before it were made.

'Far enough,' I said. But he knew that already, from the dust on our clothes. A man with a true nose for information does not have to rely on words.

'Staying long?' he asked, and his quick bright eyes turned to Gerda, to reckon up her weariness.

'That depends,' I said. 'Is this the sort of town where a man may earn a little—without breaking his back for it?'

'That depends too,' he said. 'It depends on the value you set on your words. One man's little may be plenty to another. But it's a fair town and well governed.'

His glance slid past Gerda and rested for a moment on Lothar before he turned back to me. I thought he looked sharper, less agreeable.

'But *you* should do comfortably enough,' he added. 'They say the Countess has a great liking for . . .' And there he stopped.

'A great liking for what?'

'Shall we say—beggars?' He laid his finger along the side of his nose and winked at me.

'We are not beggars,' I said, liking him less and less every minute.

'I think you understand me, brother,' he said, looking sideways at Lothar. And he winked again.

The sly suggestiveness of his manner irritated me even more than the fact he might have guessed our secret. If he knew something, or thought he knew, let him come out with it. I caught his wrist in a grip that brought the water to his eyes and made him gasp.

'I am not your brother,' I said. 'And perhaps I become stupid at sunset, for I do not understand you plainly.' Then I let him go.

'I meant only that your . . . companion . . . does not wear his cloak quite . . . as other men do,' he muttered, nursing his hurt wrist and anxious only to placate me. 'For sure, you have none of you the seeming of beggars. Indeed, your friend with the . . . crooked shoulder . . . has more the bearing of a prince . . .'

'It is a pity about his back,' I said, with a greater show of carelessness than I felt.

Lothar pushed the jug of ale aside and leaned across the table toward the pedlar.

'What you were saying about the Countess interests me,' he said. 'She is a charitable lady?'

'She is a bitch. But why let that trouble you?' The pedlar lowered his voice confidentially. 'Why eat from a wooden bowl when there's gold plate to be had . . .'

Our faithful Barney chose that instant to leap from his place at Gerda's side and to fling himself, with flapping wings and jabbing beak, at the pedlar's head, driving him to a far part of the room. Lothar looked angry and Gerda scolded, but I applauded our brave bird. Abel Oake had earned his bruises and we were better without him. The fuss soon died down; there was no real damage to repair, and we finished our supper without further incident. All the same, it seemed prudent to retire early to our outhouse, lest Barney should take exception to any others of the company.

Being used to Barney's short and jealous temper, I lost no sleep over the quarrel. I did not care what the innkeeper thought of it, for we would be leaving in the morning, whatever happened, to find ourselves a permanent lodging where Lothar might remain as secret as he wished. And if the pedlar complained, a coin or a threat would quiet him. So I slept. Gerda slept too, and so did Barney—though there was a moment in the night when I heard him cursing in the straw and, without fully waking, put my hand over his beak to hush him. It must have been then that Lothar went away, and if I had heeded Barney I might have stopped him. But I knew nothing until Gerda shook me awake, and told me that Lothar had gone.

I was still stupid with sleep. I thought she made a great ferment out of something that needed no explanation. Lothar had risen early to relieve his bladder, and to swill his head under the pump before the whole world was awake to see him.

'No,' Gerda said. 'Look!'

She opened the door and I saw the stable-yard all smothered under snow, knee-deep in snow—and there were no marks on it to show where a man had walked. The pump was a pillar of snow like the ones children heap, putting stones for eyes. No one had washed there that morning.

Gerda said, 'He did not go recently.'

A servant came out of the inn and waded through the snow, making two long channels in it, to knock packed ice from the spout and handle. In spite of the cold, the water had not frozen; he drew a pailful and went back, whistling.

'The pedlar will know something,' I said. 'But you wait here.'

She said no, she would come with me, and together we went through the spoiled snow to the inn-kitchen where a fire was already burning and our host at table, carving wedges from a huge piece of cold beef.

'This won't last,' he said, nodding toward the window. 'Too soon in the season and not cold enough. A freak fall, you might say, to remind us of what will come.'

His manner was pleasant and civil, I could find no fault with it.

'Our friend rose early,' I said. 'In fact, very early. Perhaps he left a message for us, where he may be found?'

'What friend is that?' His manner did not change, his voice was no more than mildly curious.

'Why,' I said, 'the man who was with us when we came last night. A tall man in a cloak, one shoulder higher than the other . . .'

He did not even pause for reflection.

'There was no one with you,' he said. 'Yourself, this woman— and the bird. No one else.'

'A tall man,' I told him again. 'A silent man in a long cloak . . .'

'Yourself, this woman and the bird,' he said. 'I am not so busy that I could forget. A man and a woman going together from place to place is not unusual, but I took special note of you because of the gander. A solitary gander is not the travelling-companion many choose. So I noticed you. You had food and drink, spoke to no one, and went soon to bed . . .'

Ah, that was his mistake, I thought. A dozen witnesses could be found, who would say otherwise.

'What about the pedlar?' I asked him.

And he replied, 'What pedlar?' But this time I sensed uncertainty in him. Before he spoke there had been a pause, very slight, no longer than a breath, but long enough. His eyes did not quite meet mine.

'The pedlar Barney attacked,' said Gerda, interrupting in a high, frightened voice. 'Abel Oake.'

'There was no pedlar here last night,' said the innkeeper, firmly. 'My ale is very good,' he added, as though that explained all.

We left. There was nothing to be done there, the innkeeper would have continued with his 'What friend was that?' and 'What pedlar?' throughout the day, until either one of us tired. If I had tired first I might have struck him, and ended the day in gaol. It was better to go.

'Where shall we begin to look?' Gerda said. 'And how?'

There was no answer to it. Lothar himself might have paid the innkeeper for his silence; he might have chosen, after much deliberation, to leave us there; he might not want us to find him. Or perhaps the innkeeper spoke truthfully—perhaps Gerda and I *had* travelled alone since the beginning, each accompanied by a need given separate flesh and blood but emanating from our minds, a shared delusion. But if that were so, what of the priest who had seen the archangel Gabriel in Lothar? What of the physician who had examined his wing? What of the pedlar?

'We must find the pedlar again,' I said. 'That first.'

There was a white space in my mind where Lothar had been, and I'm sure there was a like space in Gerda's heart, but these were things we would not admit, even to each other. Lothar would be found. It was a statement of fact to replace the one we had carried so long—that Lothar would be released from his enchantment. Both were determined beliefs—but impossible of proof.

For a winter day, it was a very long one. The snow melted, the sun shone out. We took a room above a carpenter's shop, establishing our claim with a month's rent, which would bring the year near Christmas. The carpenter promised me work too, if I should want it, and that was good. Then we went into the streets again, wherever people were likely to gather—the taverns, the marketplace, the city gate. No one knew of a pedlar with a bruised head.

But the gatekeeper remembered us. He asked if we had found the inn comfortable; he sent many travellers there and the host usually gave him something for his trouble. I gave him something too, to help his memory further, but it was a coin wasted. He remembered only Gerda and myself—and Barney. Not Lothar.

'Good that the snow is melted,' he said.

I said, 'What snow?'

And we went back to the carpenter's house.

For three days we combed the town, with precious little hope and no success at all. I wondered if our failure, in Lothar's case, were predetermined by the limits imposed on my questioning. No one had seen a tall hunchback with a fair, proud face—but would I have got a different response had I enquired for a handsome prince carrying the wing of a swan in place of an arm? Others beside pedlars have sharp sight—and Lothar was not always careful . . .

It is often so, as though a secret were worth nothing in itself without the spice of discovery. The man with something to hide has also, it seems, a will to be discovered, and displays his secret in hints and riddles that may be read by anyone. Lothar, among strangers, would speak of wonders and enchantments in so frank and open a way that Gerda would tremble for him—and I have sometimes thought that the gape of cloak which revealed his wing to me as I watched from under the gable was not entirely accident. Yet we, who were closest to him, had been sworn to guard his secret.

Winged man or hunchback, Lothar should have been easy to find. His beauty was singular, not to be forgotten. But Abel Oake was a different matter. The pedlar belongs to a breed that goes everywhere unremarked except by those who live in such isolated places that they can count the months between one stranger and the next. Moreover, his occupation is seasonal; when winter keeps him walled up in one town for months at a stretch, he is likely to practise some other trade until the roads are clear again. We might as well have looked for a cooper, a shoemaker or a slaughterer.

On the second day Barney left us, and Gerda had another grief to add to the loss of Lothar.

'He has flown south,' I said, trying to think what a bird might do. 'No, he has found a wife, and will come back when he tires of her.' That was better. But it would not do for Gerda. She was certain he was dead, and quietly mourned for him.

On the fourth day we gave up our search, telling each other that it was for a while only, that before long someone would bring news and, until then, we must wait. The carpenter had commissioned from me a set of carvings for the panels of an oak press and I set to work on them, making a pun of our patron's name—which was Fysshe—with a pattern of fat dolphins and slender sea-maids. Gerda, left alone, went to market for vegetables and pot-herbs. We disguised our trouble in commonsense activity, trying to pretend in this way that all was well and that we did what we did from choice.

And Gerda, without any conscious effort, without even recognizing him, found our missing pedlar. He had turned bear-ward for the winter months and was leading a poor, shambling, shaggy brute that would not dance, would not even stay upright on its hind legs for long but dropped continually on all four, swaying its head from side to side in a confused and melancholy manner while the pedlar tugged helplessly on its chain. At first the people laughed. The idea of a dancing bear which would not even shuffle was humorous. But soon they grew impatient and began to poke at the bear with sticks and staffs, and to make little rushes at it, growling ferociously, so that it was afraid and tried to hide within itself, whimpering more like a kitten than a bear. The people wanted fierceness in their entertainment. If the bear would not dance for them, let it snarl and show its teeth and behave in a bear-like way. Perhaps a stone or two, neatly aimed, would help to remind it of its nature . . .

When the stones began to fly, Gerda ran for me, having more compassion for the bear than for its master, I suspect. I do not know what she thought I could do, or what strange power she saw in me, capable of quelling an unruly crowd . . . but, fortunately, it was all over by the time we reached the market-place. The people, grown bored, had gone away, and the bear-ward was sitting on the cobbles, soothing his beast with rough pats and gentle curses. Gerda spoke to him, he looked up—and I knew him at once.

'This is well met,' I said. 'We have searched for you these three days . . .'

He did not ask why I wanted him but said simply that he had been away from town, fetching his bear from a kinsman's stable.

'A liability,' he said. 'A rug on four legs, another mouth to feed. I took him in clearance of a bad debt, and was a fool to do it.'

The bear sat back on its haunches and yawned, blinking its small eyes. Years afterwards I carved them, the sparrow-shanked, sly-eyed pedlar with his chained beast, yawning and half-asleep, in stone on the top of a column in a cathedral nave—but at this moment my only thought was for Lothar.

'Last time we met,' I said, 'you had something to say which I did not want to hear. I will listen now.'

He pulled a long face. 'Had you listened then, it might have meant a pension for me. Today, a penny. Tomorrow, nothing.'

'Not even a penny,' I told him. 'But a sore head if you do not speak.'

He left his bear at a tavern where he was lodging and came with us. Seeing how tenderly he cared for the ugly brute, I liked him better and began to trust him more. Yet it was a distinction with little difference. I had to trust him whether I liked him or not; he seemed to hold the only clue to Lothar's whereabouts, and that might be a faint one.

We gave him food and waited while he satisfied his hunger, which was truly immense.

'I starve myself for that beast,' he said, explaining his great appetite. And I think it was true. Even the worst of us loves something more than he loves himself.

'The Countess Almira has a weakness for—beggars,' I prompted.

'For the unusual,' he said. 'For whatever escapes from the night-world into this—a calf born with two heads, a boy sprouting horns or—'

'A man with a wing.'

'A wing, was it? I guessed it would be something of a rare sort. And *very* rare, I may tell you. Such prodigies are not often beautiful but, whatever your friend conceals beneath his cloak, his face itself is wonderful . . .'

'Your Countess purchases freaks,' I said, harshly. 'And you hoped to be her agent. Is that what you were telling us?'

'Yes,' he said. 'Put crudely, that is what I meant. I live by buying and selling, by dropping the right word into the right ear. I know that everything has its price and that, when the price is exact, there is no need for bargaining. You need an extra sense for judging when the time is ripe, when one party needs what the other needs to sell. I have that sense.'

I looked at his shabby clothes, and at the crumbs of our meal. Even these he did not despise but was scooping them up in his hand, to waste nothing.

'You should be a rich man,' I said.

'But that I have bad luck,' he answered. 'My own stars are against me. Yet that evening, when I saw you at the inn, I knew the time was right; your friend was as right for the Countess as she for him. The fact that he has gone to her proves it. I might have made the introduction and been rewarded. But I got nothing out of it for myself because your damned bird drove me off when I was leading to the point. Your friend, whatever he may be, is not a fool. He twigged my meaning, and side-slipped me. So I lose my pension, my poor bear has to dance for his keep, and I take the road next spring. Bad luck, nothing else.'

'How can you be so sure he has gone to the Countess?' Gerda asked.

'If he's not with you, where else would he be?'

'We have asked everywhere,' I said. 'There was a snowfall to cover his tracks, and no one had seen him . . .'

'No one had seen him at all,' said Gerda. 'Not the man at the inn, not the gatekeeper who let us into the city. No one.' She shuddered with remembered fear.

Abel brought his fist down hard on the table. 'You are not listening,' he said. 'You are not looking. You are not thinking. Have you seen the Countess, or heard anything about her?'

'We have seen her,' I said. 'And you told us yourself she is a bitch.'

'A bitch. And you would know that from seeing her. What was she like when you saw her?'

'Beautiful,' said Gerda.

'White,' I said. 'White skin, white dress, white hair. And silver eyes.'

'White as snow,' he said. 'Think, man. What does snow do?'

'Why, it freezes. It numbs . . .'

'And then it warms. A man dying of cold sinks into snow as though it were a feather-bed.'

(103)

This was common knowledge—but what had it to do with us?

'But for other men, those who will live, it numbs,' he said. 'It numbs the fingers and the feet, and it numbs the mind. The mind goes white, and blank, and forgetful. Lady Almira is not a witch—except in as far as all women are witches—but I am sure she commands the snow.'

'I am a practical man,' I said. 'Snow is not at the command of any woman.'

He gestured his contempt for my opinion.

'I too am a practical man and find certain things hard to believe—but I have seen women command the winds by tying knots in twine, and, because of what they did, ships sank and men drowned. Surely this one woman may call down a little snow, enough to make a few men forget what they have seen . . .?'

Yes, I thought, men choose what they believe. Some will tell you that a unicorn may be caught with ease when he puts his head down in a maiden's lap; and others will say that God, who made the universe in seven days, fathered a son who was a mortal man and died. Which of these two strange tales is likeliest of belief?

'Has she no man to govern her?'

Abel laughed at me. 'The Count was born under Mars, which is a war-like planet. He is forever away, fighting the French or the infidels or any other nation that can put an army in the field. Perhaps he fights his own old age as well, who knows? The Lady manages his estates—and amuses herself. She does both excellently.'

'And you think Lothar has gone to this woman?'

'I am sure of it . . .'

'But why?' cried Gerda. 'Can she make him whole?'

'In a manner of speaking,' said the pedlar. 'Yes. Perhaps your friend was tired of hiding his difference from the world, tired of chasing one healer after another, tired of walking from one town to the next like a licensed beggar, tired of waking each morning to the hopelessness of having only hope and nothing else. I told you the time was right . . . Now wait a little. Tomorrow or the next day, soon now, the whole town will buzz with news of a foreign prince come to visit the Lady—no question of a penniless traveller discovered one night at an inn, no question of that at all. Your young friend will break upon this town like the noon sun breaking through cloud. As for you, I think you will be either summoned to the castle—or sent packing. That is, if your friend remembers you, and if the Countess thinks you important.'

'Of course he will remember us,' said Gerda. But I was less certain. After all, Lothar had never invited us to go with him, never from the beginning of our travels together. He could leave us whenever he wished, whenever it suited him. He owed us nothing, not even loyalty.

'Don't rely on it,' said Abel. 'He's lying in snow now, warm and smiling.'

'We'll stay,' I said. 'However difficult it becomes, we'll stay.'

I went to the street-door with him. The sun was setting over the roof-tops and the road was as tidy now, at the end of the day, as it had been at morning. I thought, not for the first time, that this was the best-ordered city I had ever seen, and the cleanest—and it was vile.

'Better a stinking midden and a good heart,' I said.

We parted. Abel walked a few steps, turned and came back.

He said, 'I have just remembered something. Yesterday, when I came back to the city with my bear, I passed a church, the one on the hill just beyond the wall, dedicated to Saint Michael. Do you know it?'

I knew it.

'On the tower there is a niche, and in the niche a figure of Saint Michael with his foot on the Devil.'

Yes, I had noticed it the evening we came to the city. There was nothing special about the workmanship, but its position was prominent and it caught the eye.

'Yesterday,' said Abel, 'it had but one wing. Oh, it meant nothing to me at the time. Stone breaks in sudden cold, heads fall, arms snap off—so may a wing. I didn't give it another thought—till now. But I think the Lady must be serious . . .'

'To mutilate a statue in a consecrated place, she would need to be very serious,' I said. 'But you were probably right in your first thought. Stone breaks in the cold, and the figure is exposed to all weathers.'

'It was snapped off clean. There was no wing fallen on the ground, and no pieces of broken stone . . .'

'Someone cleared it away,' I said. 'It's too neat a town to leave rubble lying.'

'It's too proud a town to leave a broken statue standing. It would have been removed or mended. I think the Countess is in love.'

I kept that piece of information to myself, thinking Gerda had enough to worry her. And it meant trouble, whichever way one looked. Lothar would be flattered by the love of such a fine lady—if he thought only of her beauty. Perhaps he would even love her in return, and my sweet Gerda be forgotten—but whether he gave back love for love or not, sooner or later the old Count would come riding home, if only to get more money or men for his wars. A man devoted to fighting may be willing to overlook his lady's amusements in his absence for as long as she puts his own interests first, the management of his lands and revenue. A lady in love with her leman is another matter, she is a threat to his security—and perhaps a danger to his life. If the old Count had any sense he would kill the man his wife loved. And how could the world, which needs beautiful things, survive the loss of Lothar? I could not speak of this to Gerda.

'We have to stay,' she said, when I went back to our room. It was a statement with a question in it, a question with only one answer.

'Of course,' I said. 'Where could we go, without Lothar? But for him, you would be on your goose-green still, and I, a carver, powdered with stone dust . . .'

We had to stay in the city for Lothar's sake, because he was the entire meaning in our lives. That was enough for Gerda to know.

'We were a comfort to him, weren't we?' she insisted. 'He was glad of our company. He would have given up long ago, had he been alone . . .'

Her grief made me feel ashamed, as though it were I who betrayed her. I put my arm round her shoulders, to comfort her. And she wept all the more.

'I am weeping for myself,' she said. 'I do not deserve your comfort.'

Yet it is always for ourselves we weep, however we attempt to disguise it. Grief in another rouses our anger rather than our tears, anger at the cause, at the bitter waste of pain that can do no good. Now I was angry with Lothar. I would have hated him, had that been possible.

'It was a dream,' she said. 'Never anything else. I thought he would look at me one day—the way a man looks at a girl. I was glad when it was cold and when the wind blew. I was glad when my feet were swollen and blistered. I was glad because I thought he would remember it, that I had suffered so much for his sake, and that he would love me for it.'

'You cannot buy love with pain,' I said.

The next day, just as Abel had foretold, the streets were full of gossip concerning the Lady's new lover—gossip and bawdy jokes and whispers. By evening there was a new song made, which was heard everywhere:

> In autumn when the leaves were red
> And the evening cold did sting,
> A handsome lord to his lady sped,
> And she welcomed him to her feather bed
>   Where he covered her . . .
>
> He covered her with his wing.
>
> The young lord to the castle gate
> His trailing plumes did bring.
> The Lady welcomed him with state
> And knew at last she had found her mate
>   When he covered her . . .
>
> He covered her with his wing.

It seemed there were a thousand verses, variations of the first, each with the same refrain, not subtle but very insistent. In every tavern people drank the health of the Countess and long life to her new lover who was half a bird. Lothar had caught the imagination of the city; they delighted in him.

Gerda suffered terribly, but I suffered too. The God with whom I vied for mastery in our shared craft, had shown me perfection. He had let me travel beside it for a while, and now had taken it away from me and given it to a whore instead. It was a cruel slight.

But we stayed—because of Lothar. And I do not suppose he cared very much whether we stayed or went. He was, as our friend the pedlar had said, asleep in the snow—and smiling.

We saw him from time to time, accompanying the Countess on

horseback, and now he wore his wing carelessly, like a great white cloak tossed back from his shoulder, the feathers brushing his horse's rump and driving the beast mad with their touch, so that it skittered sideways on the stones, dancing and tossing its head while its eyes rolled fearfully. The Countess rode close to him, and her eyes never left his face. It seemed that the gaze of each was mingled with that of the other, as the limbs of lovers are entwined and, as in love one eats and one is eaten, so the Countess Almira devoured Lothar—and he was content to let it be.

I wondered if they knew what the town was singing. Every day there were different verses—but they were all the same:

> The Lady lay within her bower
> And toyed with her wedding ring,
> She called to her lover at the midnight hour
> And opened her arms like a lily flower
> And he covered her . . .
>
> He covered her with his wing.

I found myself whistling it as I worked at the carpenter's bench. Abel's bear, though he would not dance, swung his head to and fro to that particular rhythm.

Gerda still thought of nothing but Lothar. Her days were filled with the pain both of seeing him, and of not seeing him.

'Why was *I* not born a lady?' she demanded. 'Then he could have loved me, without disgrace . . .'

I hated to hear her belittle herself, it was worse to me than her tears.

'I called you "lady" once, do you remember? But it was wrong of me. You are a goose-girl,' I said. 'And that is better than any lady. But, Gerda, did you ever hear of the goose-girl who was really a princess?' I struggled to recall the old story. 'She was on her way to marry a king, but the servant took her place and she was sent to herd geese on a high, windy common . . .'

'And what happened?'

'It ended well,' I said. 'Stories of enchantment always end well, or no one would listen. But think of a useless princess, who had never so much as brushed her own hair, coping with four-score geese and a few arrogant ganders, each one of them with a will of its own? A lady is all very well to look at, Gerda, but you would not care to be one.'

'I miss poor Barney,' she said. So, thinking it would please her, I carved a gander, to take his place, as my wooden cat had taken the place of the real one I had loved. She accepted it and smiled but I saw that it made her sad rather than otherwise.

'No, it is not the same,' I said. 'Put it on the fire.'

She would not do that, but sat with it in her hands, not speaking.

A few days later, Barney himself returned, with an air of very well-fed importance, but he only stayed an hour or two, then he was gone.

'What did I tell you?' I said. 'He has found a wife. There will be goslings soon, with big grey feet like his, and short tempers.'

The pedlar, Abel, was visiting us at the time; he frequently came in the evenings to see how we did and to give us sound advice which we always ignored, since his one idea was that we should leave the city before the winter ice set in, making the roads unusable. He had forgotten his old quarrel with Barney, and said, offhandedly, 'Ah, that bird's back,' as though it were something we should have expected, not an occasion for celebration.

When he next came he said, 'I've found out where your gander keeps himself these days. He's gone to live at the castle with your winged friend. Like staying with like, I reckon.'

I told him that Barney had never cared for Lothar.

'No more do I,' said Abel. 'His sort should stay between the covers of a book, or on a bit of tapestry. Walking the world, they're a temptation to honest folk . . .'

I thought that nonsense and said so.

'A temptation to dream,' he insisted. 'To open the shutters and let the night in. Your gander doesn't like him because he smells of trouble. A bird should be all bird, thinks the gander. And a man should be all man, say I.'

Gerda said gently that Lothar was not to blame for his predicament.

'I don't like his story either,' said Abel. 'I get about the countryside in the travelling season, as you know, and I have nowhere heard of a duchess condemned to be burned as a witch and saved at the last minute by eleven swans who turned into proper young men, all except one.'

'Nevertheless, it is true,' I said.

'So it may be—but I have heard it nowhere else. Perhaps it happened oversea, in some other country . . .'

'No,' I said. 'I knew of the dumb duchess long ago, before ever I met Lothar.'

'A dumb duchess, yes, maybe. But *eleven* brothers changed to swans? That I would have heard, had it happened within a thousand leagues. The country would be ringing with such a story. That is what I mean about letting the night in. When a man who, by all the laws of creation, should not exist, steps from his world into ours, everything changes.'

'Yes,' I said. 'He makes his own laws as he goes along, his own past, his own people . . .'

I spoke without thinking. Having thought, I said, 'No, if that were the way it is, I would have to doubt your existence— and my own. I think Lothar told us his story truly, as it happened. It is because your mind is closed that you cannot accept him.'

But I remembered how the earth had tried to shrug him off, turning her year back in an endeavour to reach a place and time where he was not; I remembered how the air had refused to hold him, and flung him to the earth again . . .

'As you like,' said Abel. 'Whatever he is, he's better at the castle. They're all strange up there.'

'And enchantment is a thing of the past,' said Gerda, wryly.

'I wish with all my heart it were,' said Abel. 'But I have met too much that cannot be otherwise explained. I see too much. I hear too much. Enchantment is still with us—and I travel with a piece of iron in my pack, because I am afraid. I do not want the night let in.'

'Lord Lothar hates his wing,' said Gerda. 'He wants only to be as other men.'

'Listen,' said Abel. 'On the other side of the country I heard of a parish priest who left his house and his hearth-companion, his own children and all his flock of souls—because one day the Archangel Gabriel came to him in his church and ordered him to change his ways. On that same day, they told me, three strangers came to the village, something that happens so rarely it is never forgotten. The priest himself said there were only two, who had come to arrange a wedding. His woman also saw two, but she thought it was something else, not a wedding, brought them there—'

'What happened to the priest?'

'He goes from place to place, preaching repentance. Most people say he is mad.'

'He was a good man,' I said. 'If anyone ever deserved a visit from an angel, that man did.'

'There is more to come,' said Abel. 'Not far from there, a drunken reeve awakened on a hillside where he had stumbled astray the night before. He looked toward the sunrise and saw, quite clearly, Lucifer. Lucifer, the fallen son of the morning, standing between earth and sky, with one of his great wings spread and flaming. He was holding out his hands, the reeve said, to receive the sinful world.'

'And what happened to the reeve?'

'He became devout,' said Abel. 'He is known far and wide for his sober and just dealings.'

'Then Lord Lothar has done nothing but good,' Gerda said. 'Both these people were changed for the better.'

'They saw what they had need to see, their own souls turned inside out, perhaps. For some this could be dangerous—to others as well as to themselves. What did you see?'

'Sorrow,' said Gerda.

'And feathers,' said Abel. 'Nothing strange to you, who were brought up with birds. Perhaps you needed sorrow to show you what contentment is.'

I remembered that I had thought something similar about my goose-girl Virgin, the one the Dean had so much disliked. That beauty needed grief to make it complete.

'And you?' Abel asked me.

'I saw Lothar,' I said.

'Indeed,' said Abel, flatly. 'You saw Lothar. But somewhere I heard of a marvellous craftsman, who could make birds so true that they sang in their stone. He went away, saying he would be back, but he has not been seen since, and not heard of.'

'Only God can make birds that sing,' I said. 'But what of yourself? You too have seen Lothar.'

'When I see something that has wandered from its own world, I touch my piece of iron. That protects me.'

'The wind blows—and pedlars talk,' I said. 'Thank you for bringing news of the gander.'

A few weeks later, he brought other news.

'Forget your friend,' he said. 'The old Count has been taken prisoner.'

I confessed I did not see the connection. He was very patient with me, explaining that the Count was offered for ransom; on the payment of so much money he would be released.

'Well?'

'The Countess will not treat for him. If her lord is in prison, he will stay in prison. In a little while he will die. I told you—she is serious.'

'Then we must wait,' I said. 'And see what will happen. As far as it goes, the situation is better than it was. In prison the Count may live for years—in battle he might have died at any day . . .'

'And he might have returned at any day. Now there is no restraint at all, the Countess already regards herself as free.'

No restraint! I had not noticed her greatly restrained before.

Abel found me very innocent.

'The town doesn't care a fart for the Count. He's never here except to grind out a tax or two to pay for his weapons and his horses—and to persuade able-bodied men away from the plough. When the Count comes home, belts are tightened and women claim to be widows while their husbands lie hid from him. But they all love the Lady. She brings trade to the town and gives feasts and junketings for them. Why, man, they're even proud of her lovers . . .'

It was quite true. That very evening, bonfires were kindled in the surrounding hills, and an ox roasted at the castle gate. When the Countess appeared, walking among the people, her hand on Lothar's arm, the crowd cheered her.

Passing an open door on my road home, I heard the new verse they had added to their interminable, damnable song:

> A messenger rode to the castle keep
> And merry news did bring.
> The old Count held in a dungeon deep,
> Had languished there since spring.
> The Lady turned to her lover in her sleep
>   And he covered her. . .
>
>   He covered her with his wing.

I felt sick with shame, sick to the roots of my being. And I was reminded, curiously, of the carved Christ the old priest had shown me when he took me away from the woods. I had the same sense of something lovely spoiled.

Gerda was late home and I was afraid for her safety in the riotous streets. People were dancing now and, in my imagination, I saw her caught up in it, whirled round and round, passed from one pair of sweaty hands to another, while her heart was breaking.

But she was smiling when she came in. Gerda smiling! I could not believe it.

She said, 'Matthew, I went to the church—'

'And that made you smile?'

It would have made me weep to go into a church on such a day, to go into the house of a God who had left off caring.

'And look what I found,' she said, holding out her hand to show me what was in it. It was a feather, a white swan's feather.

'Lord Lothar must have been there earlier. Perhaps he went to pray for the Count's safety . . .'

'Or his own,' I said.

'It doesn't matter which. Matthew, have you ever known Lord Lothar go into a church—except that one time? If he can pray, there's hope for him—'

I wanted to believe it—but I had stood very close to Lothar at the ox-roasting. I was so close that I could smell the scent on his crimped and curling hair—and he did not look to me like a man who had come recently from a church. If Gerda had found a feather near the altar, as she said, then someone else must have put it there—someone who wished him well and hoped that the offering of a feather might put him under God's protection. It was the sort of thing Gerda herself might have done—but she had not . . .

Barney, I thought. Who else so close to Gerda, he would think with her mind, do as she would have done?

So Barney had not deserted us merely for the sake of silk pillows and a rich diet, as had seemed the case, but to further our own cause by keeping watch on Lothar. A noble, unselfish bird. I smiled at Gerda, sharing her delight, but keeping my thoughts to myself.

I have always liked the winter months, sharp cold in the air and the earth sleeping and, even in this hateful city, so clean and glittering on the surface and festering beneath, I felt the same warm pleasure in the approach of Christmas as I had known in other years. At Christmas I could even forgive God.

Gerda went out with the other young women to gather holly-boughs and ivy for the decking of the church, and came back with her cheeks glowing again, almost the old Gerda, her head filled with women's nonsense about good luck and bad, whether discarded holly should be burned or buried, kept or thrown away in the woods. Where I lived, I told her, sprigs were left in the cowsheds so that the beasts would thrive in the coming year—yet when sickness came some still throve and some died, the holly notwithstanding. Perhaps not all the sprigs had been taken from the church, Gerda said. That would account for it.

Working side by side with the carpenter, I brightened the colours of some wooden beasts to stand by Christ's crib in the nave of Saint-Michael-on-the-Hill. The crib, a pretty piece of work all carved and gilded, had been brought back from Italy by the old Count, more than thirty years before, and set up in the church each Christmas since. Handling the figures—kings, shepherds and angels—I thought of the Count in his prison and wondered if his mind, at this holy season, turned to home. He must have cared for it once, to have carried all this with him, so many pieces and so far. In those days he would be called the young Count, I supposed, and the city loud with welcome whenever he came riding in. And now he was despised. It was his Lady who presided over the feast, gave the Christchild's dole and paid the mummers. The people, though they spoke coarsely of her, held her in esteem; they made a jest of his captivity. The world was widdershins.

Together the carpenter and I wrapped the figures in cloth and stacked them in his cart, ready for taking to the church.

'They'm funny old things,' he said. 'Hardly worth the keeping from year to year . . .' He held up one of the kings, a bucolic red-cheeked character with a high spiky crown, newly repaired. 'Not handsome, properly speaking, but like himself, stiff-like.'

I asked if the carpenter remembered the old Count well. I was curious to know what sort of a man had been so rash as to ally himself, indivisibly, with such as the Lady Almira.

'Aye,' he said. 'Pretty well. Liked a quiet sort of show, nothing gaudy. Strict about Lent, he was, and hard on those who forgot to honour the Lord's day. "God before harvest"—I've heard him say that a dozen times.'

'I like the simple customs myself,' I said, swaddling an angel.

'They'm well enough.'

In three words he dismissed them, all the uncomplicated, heart-warming things—yet he was a very decent fellow in his own way, honest in business and a good craftsman when sober.

'Now, his Lady's one for pageantry,' he said. 'She can make a tourney out of a cock-fight, she's so fine, but she don't ever forget that humble folk want strong ale and fire-eaters, wrestlers and tug-o'-wars and tumblers along wi' the conjuring, fortune-telling and such-like wizardry that's to her own taste. When the Lady makes display, there's summat for everyone, and all as neat and well-turned as a scholard's argyment. But when her lord be at home, she'm like a peacock on a midden, all her fine feathers wasting . . .'

While he spoke he wedged the infant Christ head downward in the cart, and packed him in with straw.

'She'm rare,' he said. 'And—to the point, Matthew—she'm a good patron.'

I did not doubt it. Her Christmas entertainment would be a great spectacle, that was certain, and in costliness as far removed from the homely revels of other places as a cathedral is removed from a hermit's cell. In costliness, if not in kind.

I recalled earlier Christmastides spent here and there. Not least in the wretched village where I had starved out my boyhood, the visit of the Christmas mummers had been an excitement to antici-pate almost from the first fall of leaves in autumn, and to think of for weeks afterward when my famished days and nights were consoled by the memory of the white bread and roasted meat doled out at the manor house.

Christmas was always green and berry-red, winter ale and rough horse-play, fire and a full belly, twelve rich days rescued from the long lean months of cold. It had very little to do with the birth of God. Mummings and mysteries, boy bishops and lords of misrule—every town and hamlet held to its own tradition, more pagan than Christian, and none the worse for that. I had enjoyed them all.

Yet I looked forward to a part of this feast with some misgiving.

It was the custom here for the townspeople to rehearse a play or dramatic interlude for their Lady's amusement, an undertaking kept secret from all save the actors who, for some time past, had been whetting their neighbours' appetites with winks and whispers, nudges and sudden bellows of laughter. I could not avoid the suspicion that a thing so tailor-made to the Lady's liking might have more cruelty in it than I had stomach for.

Abel had similar fears but his were not confined to the play alone. He had been trying to teach his bear to stand on its head and, after a great expenditure of patience and honeycomb, had at last persuaded the brute to perform a sort of clumsy bow with one hind leg raised in the air—but this feat, of which both were justly proud, was not to be displayed at the Christmas games as Gerda and I had hoped.

'Some wit might take it into his head to throw a torch,' he said. 'And a bear with his coat on fire dances, I can tell you, even so stupid a fellow as mine. Standing on his head like this, he'd be at a disadvantage, a-blaze before he knew it. I'd sooner see a man burn, any day.'

Such things, shameful as they are, happen everywhere now and then. Drink, which makes cheerful company of most, brings out the devil in some. And the Devil, I guessed, might be found very near the surface in this city.

'A lot depends on the Lady's mood,' said Abel. 'If she's happy—and she's happy now, I grant you—all goes well. But if she's jaded, or expecting her lord home, it takes an edged jest to make her laugh. So a lot depends on the play too. If it goes slow or hangs heavy, someone or something pays. No, cully, I won't risk my bear.'

I wondered whether I dare risk myself—or Gerda. Perhaps it

would be as well to stay indoors on that day of the twelve, but our friend said no, it would be a shame to miss the spectacle. We would be safe enough in the crowd, as long as I was careful to pick no quarrel. There was little fear of that—I am not a quarrelsome man except where my art is troubling me—so we arranged to meet in an ale-booth on Saint Stephen's Day and go, the three of us together, to the acting-place where I had, a few days earlier, helped the carpenter to erect a palisade and several scaffolds.

The Place was a great field immediately below the castle and adjoining the city wall. From the castle which, at this quarter, shared its wall with the city, a private door led direct to the high dais where the Countess and her court sat, opposite to the largest of the acting-scaffolds and level with it. Both dais and scaffold were hung with cloth of crimson and gold, and each had two thrones with canopies. Neither dais nor scaffold was more splendid than the other. The lesser stages, two on either side, were canopied with green boughs—holly, ivy and laurel—and hung with cloth dyed crimson to match the others, but of a homelier texture. The whole scene was lit by several score of torches and, I dare say, it had a cheerful and festive look—but not to me . . .

The crowd was excited and must have made some noise . . . yet I heard nothing. It was like the silence before an earth tremor. What I saw might have been a picture painted on cloth or on a wall, so vivid a representation that one says how real it looks, which one would not say if it looked real at all. That is a paradox. This scene looked real but I was not, at that time, deceived by its seeming reality. I knew it for a picture. There was a certain flatness of perspective, a distancing between myself and what I saw. I was not part of it then.

The Countess Almira and Lothar were seated on their twin thrones, side by side, each half-turned to look into the other's face but not smiling as lovers do. One was the mirror image of the other, and the smile a man directs toward his mirror is not quite the same as the one he offers his love. They were both dressed in white, Lothar's wing hanging like a sleeve curiously cut to hide the arm and hand. And the Lady's gown had one sleeve cut to the same pattern, like a wing.

Gerda gasped and whispered, 'O, but that's dreadful!' Indeed, it was most subtle and perverse—my skin tingled as though it were touched with ice—but it was bold too, the way the Lady flaunted her infatuation for Lothar.

'It is very beautiful!' I said. 'Give her that.'

A man with a gold chain round his neck and a baton in his hand walked to the centre of the Place and raised his hands for silence. He looked very stately, like a mayor or alderman, but it was only Will Dodd the Tanner, a great nowt, cuckolded four times a year, on quarterday, so it was said. Now he beckoned a youth from the crowd, a lad plainly dressed in tunic and hood, and introduced him as Mortal Man, for whose soul the vices and virtues would contend before he achieved his just reward . . .

Ha! I thought, a moral interlude—an unlikely entertainment for the Lady!

But this was morality turned hind-end-foremost. The central scaffold was occupied not by God but by Lady Lechery, one of the town harlots dressed in a white gown that had once belonged to the Countess, and wearing a flaxen wig. At her shoulders stood Worldly-Wise—that is, the father of Lechery—and the Devil, very handsome in a bishop's mitre, with a long barbed tail parting his cope at the back.

Will Dodd explained it all. Mortal Man, having been tempted by the virtues, severally and together, was to win through to the good fellowship of Worldly-Wise and marriage with his daughter. The Devil, said Will Dodd, would officiate. He bowed low and resigned his place to the actors.

The play was under way. Mortal Man began his earthly journey, to be assailed in turn by Chastity, Wise Counsel, Piety and Humility . . . but what unattractive virtues were these, such as might tempt only the most abject fool. Every one of them was held up to ridicule, and then twisted to show an underbelly of self-seeking which made all seem vicious. Having failed to tempt Mortal Man from his broad path to Hell—and that largely through incompetence—each in turn was overthrown by the servants of Worldly-Wise, conventional vices, and all ended in the Lady's wedding party, rioting together.

Thus Chastity, another whore, with a round red face and sooty eyebrows, quickly fell victim to Lust, a merry fellow who wagged a goat's tail at the end of his rump. Wise Counsel, a foolish old man in a doctor's gown, listened open-mouthed to Bribery and discarded his ass-ears for an astrologer's cap embroidered all round with the signs of the zodiac. And Piety, whose long sanctimonious face and mispronounced Latin had been greeted with laughter so prolonged that it brought the play to a halt, hitched up the skirts of his monk-like habit and danced a lewd jig, arm in arm with Blasphemy and Sacrilege, while Humility, a cringing beggar, filled the bag he carried round his neck with coins tossed to him by the nobility on the dais.

It was well done and would have been very, very funny, I think, but for the sneer I sensed in it. The fun was not kindly meant, but barbed like the Devil's tail. The Lady loved it. And so did the people. They stamped their feet, they laughed, they howled for more. In the red torchlight, they were like devils themselves, their eyes wet, their mouths loose and slobbering. Some even wore devil-masks, but these were innocent beside the real faces of those around us.

Perhaps it is as hard to describe true evil as it is true virtue. When one sees it, one knows, though it be garbed in commonplace. We may speak familiarly of the Devil, calling him Old Scratch, belittling him with hearth-warm tenderness, saying, 'We bean't afeard o' he!' and meaning it—but we should never forget that we are dealing with the Prince of Dark. When we call him, though it be in frolic, he comes. And he was there, at the Lady's Christmas revels.

'We must get Gerda away,' I said, turning to where Abel had stood no more than a moment since. But the press of the crowd had separated us and I could see neither of my friends. I hoped they had contrived to stay together . . .

. . . Chastity, with a great pillow stuffed under her petticoats, tumbled down the steps of her scaffold to grab at the ankles of Mortal Man who in his turn was ogling Lady Lechery. Mortal Man, now wearing a fine fur hat over his hood, and a velvet cloak over his tunic, kicked her in the belly and pranced on. Chastity got to her feet, pummelled the pillow into place, and lurched away in pursuit of Lust, screaming with laughter that could not be heard for the louder laughter of those who watched.

The noise was now so great that all words were lost in it—but the players made their meaning clear by grossly exaggerating every gesture. The torches flared and smoked. The watchers surged to and fro, in search of better vantage points. It was like a vast sea made solid. Waves of it broke through onto the actors' ground and were pushed back again. Fights began, but came to nothing. Ale-jacks passed from hand to hand. I was no longer able to determine my own movement, but let myself be shoved here and there, wherever there was a space large enough to admit me, wherever the crowd parted for a moment or was still. Was this how I came to be at the edge of the acting-space—and then inside it? I do not remember—except that I was there—whether I were pushed, propelled or dragged. Hands caught mine and whirled me round while I struggled to get free of them; I tripped and was pulled along on my knees until other hands hauled me to my feet again. A Fool in a cap with bells struck me on the head with his inflated pig's bladder and a voice hissed in my ear, 'Tha's Truth. He'll turn 'ee right-side up, surely.'

I was in a circle of spinning faces—not the faces of men but of apes, wolves, bats. The hands that clutched me were not hands but claws. Voices howled, chattered, brayed, squeaked. I heard my own voice howling among them—but it was with pain.

Fat Chastity jigged in front of me, her face running sweat and her round breasts bouncing. 'Why,' she said. 'Don't 'ee mind it. 'Tes only fun!' But her voice was that of the witch-i'-the-wall who had plagued me with lascivious thoughts of Gerda, and I fled from her.

Colours assaulted my eyes, searing them—red, purple, green, gold and red again. Red—and red and red. Hell was never redder or more hot than this . . . yet beyond the circle of torches, beyond the pallisade I had helped to build, the night was black, deep black and cold beyond belief. I longed to rest my eyes in that black and looked up to see snow-flakes falling—a few and very slow. Snow-flakes as big as stars, sweet as sugar on my tongue.

My mind cleared a little. I remembered something the carpenter's wife had told me. She had been working in the castle kitchens, helping to prepare the feast, and the cook had shown her the great confection of spun sugar he was making . . .

'Lovely 'tis. That prince wi' the wing, him who's sniffing round the Lady, and all in sugar, a'most as big as the man hisself. I never seed sech a thing . . .'

But why was that important? Why think of it now? The snow was sugar melting on my tongue . . . no, it was falling faster now, and more soft, not sugar but feathers falling. White feathers drifting down the sky . . .

Then I was in front of the dais and through the fine spray of floating feathers I could see the Lady and Lothar, both gloriously winged, their single hands clasped together. The Lady's eyes were closed and her mouth smiled. I thought, she is afraid Lothar will see me and remember. She is conjuring her magic snow to wrap him round, to be sure he will forget again. I called his name. I bellowed it.

'LOTHAR!'

I used my whole strength to halt the circling dance there, where I stood, to make him look at me.

'LOTHAR!'

And he turned his head, but blindly. I saw his eye-lids with white frost on them, and his eyes silvered, overlaid with ice. There was snow in my mouth, my lungs filled with feathers and I think, in that moment, I lost consciousness.

The events that followed I know only from what I was told by various people, a neighbour who brought Gerda to me, and Chastity who, I think, may have saved my life.

I awakened in a cold, dark place with the sound of water running nearby. I smelled damp stone and smoke and something I could not identify—a sweetish, rancid smell which, though unpleasant, was at the same time vaguely comforting. Again, my head was pillowed on something soft but I could not be sure what it was; there was a thick fold of cloth under my cheek but the shape was awkward and did not feel like anything I remembered. My consciousness returned slowly, a little at a time, advancing and retreating. I heard the water clearly, and separated the mingled smells one from the other, but my mind neither made nor attempted the connecting link between the past—which I had forgotten—and the present, which I could not recognize. The future had no possible existence for me. I drifted away again on the sound of the water.

When I came back my senses were, this time, concentrated in my hand, not in my head. I could feel it heavy and inert on the end of what must have been my arm though the arm itself was not included in the area of awareness. I tried to move my fingers but there was something restricting their free movement. The effort was too great, so I let the deeper dark take me again.

The next advance brought thought and I knew that another hand held mine, somewhere in a damp stone place. I tried to speak but the gap between my brain and my tongue would not close. The hand holding mine increased its pressure, and a hoarse, kindly voice—very far away—said, 'Hush 'ee now. Lie still.'

It was my mother, the witch-i'-the-wall, come back for me at last. She had not meant to leave me in the wood, merely forgotten for a while that I was there. I burrowed my head closer into her lap and thought, 'It does not matter; it was only yesterday.'

Then, very soon after that, there were other voices and a lantern.

The hoarse voice said, 'He stirred a moment back, and again just afore 'ee came . . .'

Another, light and breathless, 'Shall I hold him now?'

'No. Leave him be, to come of hisself. Thass right, sit by there, with the lantern on 'ee . . .'

'Was he . . . is he . . . much hurt?'

'Nowhere, missus. 'Twas all inside, seemingly.'

Another voice, and another. Men's voices, very low. Furry. No words. Sound of water, smell of damp. Dark.

'He's sleeping easier now . . .'

I was broad awake, stiff and very cold. Thoughts came to me, one after the other, in good order. I remembered spinning in a wild dance in the acting-place, and feathers falling. No, not feathers. Snow. I knew that my head was lying in a woman's lap and that the same woman held my hand. There was a lantern near and I saw, dimly, wet stone walls stained with green, and a low curved roof like a vault—which told me that I lay under the arch of a bridge by a stream or river. Then I shifted my dull head and . . . there was Gerda, with Abel beside her, and another man, the neighbour who had led them with his lantern.

Gerda saw my eyes open and said 'Thank God!' but she was weeping as though I were already dead and laid out for burial. Abel patted her and stroked her hair.

'Never mind God,' he said. 'Thank our Molly, here.'

'God too,' said Molly, whose lap still cradled me. I sat up, which started a plunging, throbbing pain in my head, so that I had to close my eyes again.

'Will you tell me what happened,' I said, when I could speak. 'And where I am. And why.'

'We lost you,' said Gerda. 'So Abel took me home, and went back to look for you. Much later, Tom Togood came, and brought us here.'

'You are all to be thanked,' I said. 'But why here?'

''Twas as far as we could carry 'ee,' said Molly. 'You'm no little weight. 'Tis out o' the weather, any road.'

Gerda added that they had not been allowed to take me home to our room above the carpenter's shop.

'The gate is barred. They would not let you into the city.'

'Is it leprosy then?' I cried. 'Or the pestilence again? You must keep away.' I would have staggered into the open, had I been stronger, but Molly's hand restrained me.

'No,' she said. ''Twas the Countess. She were angry because 'ee spoiled her play, and she'm not a good 'un to cross.'

I lifted the lantern and held it so that I could see her face. The pain in my head set zig-zag lines before my eyes, such as you may find round the doors of old buildings, and I had to concentrate my sight between these lines before I could see clearly.

'Do 'ee mind me, now?' she asked. 'I were Chastity in the moral play.'

She looked an even more bedraggled Chastity now, with clothes all rumpled, and the sooty black of her eyebrows smudged, hardly at all like the cheerful lump who had romped with Lust on the wooden stage.

'It were a grand play too,' she said. 'And no wonder the Countess were angry. 'Ee'd 'a been in gaol but for me speaking up for 'ee and saying 'twas the ale and nobbut else made 'ee mad . . .'

'What did I do?'

Tom Togood had seen the start.

'Thee were mutterin' to theeself, wild-like, in the crowd, and seemed not to like the play. Then thee said, quite loud, "God did not make men move for this! 'Tis blasphemy!" Well, Blasphemy were down under the scaffold, havin' a bit o' rest—so one o' the lads emptied 'is ale-pot on thy head, to cool 'ee down, like, and 'appen that were wrong thing to do. It made 'ee worse, if owt . . .'

'Worse?'

'More restless, like. 'Ee wouldn't stay still and watch like a decent quiet man, but kept shovin' through the crowd, and lookin' about . . .'

'I was looking for Gerda, certainly. But I thought the crowd shoved me.'

'And so they did, but that were later. I lost sight of 'ee for a bit. Next thing, 'ee were in the Place, among the players.'

'The crowd were getting merry, by that,' said Molly. 'They was more'n a few down in th' Place, dancing and drinking. It added to the fun and no one fretted—but you misliked it so. Then they made

sport of 'ee, and that weren't right. I thought I'd get 'ee out by
under the scaffold and I tried to soothe 'ee, saying summat, but 'ee
howled like a dog wi' his throat cut.'

'I think I remember that,' I said.

'Well, best forget what 'ee said next. If men have sportive
bodies, 'twas God made 'em so, not me. Then 'ee pulled away and
got caught up wi' some as was dancing in a ring. When 'ee came to
where the Countess were, 'ee stopped, and seemed to come over all
foggy. Thought she were Lady Lechery—but that were Bet in an
old dress the Countess give her for the acting . . .'

'I called the Countess Lady Lechery?'

'Oh, she'd not mind that. It was when 'ee grabbed at the young
lord she called her men . . .'

'Grabbed at him, did I? Grabbed at Lothar?'

'Why,' said Tom Togood. 'Thy hand were all twisted in's
feathers afore they got 'ee held, and shoutin' 'is name in 'is face, fit
to deafen 'un.'

'Was that when it snowed?'

'It never snowed,' said Molly. 'Not last night, though 'tis sleet-
ing now.'

'It never snowed,' I said. 'What then?'

'She ordered for 'ee to be locked up. And that were sad, I
thought, on Christmastide. So I pleaded for 'ee—and Lady
Lechery—our Bet—she pleaded too—and the end was the Countess said 'ee might go free. But right free, she meant, not back 'ome.
And all the time 'ee were flicing about 'ee like a windmill, and
roaring about for that Lord Lothar to help 'ee—and him standing
like stone, saying nothing. So one o' the men give 'ee a tap wi' his
cudgel and down 'ee went. Lord, master, 'ee must have a thin skull.
Well, I had to take 'ee somewhere, and the gates were barred, so
Tom Togood helped to carry 'ee this far. And I stayed with 'ee
while he went back and fetched your missus and Abel here.'

'It's a bad business at this time of year,' said Abel. 'But it might
have been worse.'

'As long as you're quite well again,' said Gerda, 'what matters?'

Tom Togood peered out at the weather, sighed heavily, and
blew on his hands.

'And I'll be gettin' 'ome,' he said, without much eagerness. 'Th' sleet's easin' now. Nay, lad, keep my cloak till we bring 'ee thy own things here . . . I'll have my lantern though, for my woman'll miss that, certain. Bist comin', Abel? Moll?'

'Will she've missed thee, Tom?'

'Eh, I'll tell 'er summat,' he said. And Molly gave a great hearty laugh that brought a breath of sanity and sweet humour into our cramped space.

'Not the truth, mind, Tom,' she said, still laughing. 'Never let on 'ee've spent half the night wi' Moll and no money changed hands—or the whole town'll be out for the same charity!'

I stood in the rain and watched our three friends go—good friends all—back to the city and the round of their lives, Abel to his bear, Moll to her bawdy and Tom Togood to his idleness. In my mind I had often disparaged Tom for a lazy scatterling and thought his wife served him well with her hard tongue—but he had spent his time and spoiled his pleasure for our sakes, or perhaps for Moll's. I vowed that in future, if there should be a future, I would be more sparing of judgement.

Now they were gone. I stooped under the arch to Gerda, where she sat on the bare earth, patient and uncomplaining as always. There is a mincing dishonesty in what poets say of weariness, it is never beautiful. The stains beneath Gerda's eyes were grey—not blue or violet. She looked bruised.

'Gerda,' I said. 'I do not know what happened back there—except that for a while I was in Hell. I can only say that I am sorry . . .'

'It was not your fault,' she said. That was true, but neither was it the fault of any other; therefore it had to stay with me.

'Well, then, fault or not, the outcome is the same. We are homeless, Gerda, because of me. The bridge was a good shelter for one night, and may keep the weather off for another day—but we cannot live through the winter under a bridge. We must think what to do.'

We had to think—yet thinking was no use. No one can feed two extra bellies in wintertime, even when it means four extra hands to work. There is no work in winter. Even if there were food and work and shelter to be had, no one would dare to take us in for fear of the

Lady's anger. We could make for another town, but this would mean leaving Lothar. I could throw myself on the Lady's mercy. The very thought was enough to make a man laugh on the road to his hanging.

Thinking forward was no use.

Thinking back, though easier, was worse. My mind kept returning, of its own, to the unlucky night that had brought us here.

'Was I bewitched? The play was an ugly thing, mocking at virtue—but I have seen many ugly things. I once saw a poor fellow in the pillory, a mewing noddy who could never have understood what he did or what men did to him—and that made me angry, Gerda, but it did not make me mad . . .'

'Perhaps we are all bewitched,' she said. Perhaps we were. Perhaps this dreary place in which we found ourselves had no reality except in our own image-making minds. I touched the green-stained stones and, touching them, tried to believe that I sat in a panelled room, with my legs stretched out in front of a fire. My belief was not strong enough.

'Lothar did not see me,' I said. 'He heard my voice—it would have wakened the most obstinate sleeper—and I think he turned his face to me. But he did not see. Gerda, I thought there was ice on his eyes . . .'

'It was the light. He may not have known you among so many . . .'

Gerda slept, her cloak folded beneath her, Tom Togood's cloak above to keep her warm. In shadow and sleep the tired lines were smoothed out and she looked young again, the way I had seen her once, when her geese were all round her, and the sun shining. One hand lay beside her head, a strong square hand, half-open, generous . . . a hand to carve.

Why, I thought, if I were making an effigy for a woman's tomb, I would make it thus—not stiff and stately, but a woman asleep with her kind hands open, relinquishing life. And a voice, which may not have been God's voice, said, 'That's right, Matthew, carve the dead. You would not expect *them* to move.'

Much later, Abel came, carrying my threadbare cloak to exchange for Tom's, and Gerda's basket with provisions in it. He forgot nothing. And, while Gerda slept and I made sculptures in my head, he had been busy on our behalf. He had solved our problem. We were to go to the church, he told us, that same church outside the walls, where Saint Michael stood, mutilated, in his niche.

'I've arranged it with the parson,' he said. 'He'll not bother you.'

Not bother us! A strange phrase to use in such circumstances. Saint Michael's had no sanctuary grant, I knew; we would be there only of the priest's courtesy and must, therefore, have dealings with him in some sort. He would want to hear our confessions and bring us to repentance, that being a part of his duty toward God. But he would also need to keep the favour of the Countess, since his living depended on it—and how might he do this while he sheltered us?

'He sees the dilemma, and thinks it best not to know certainly that you are there. Or, if he cannot avoid so knowing, better not to know who you are. If you keep out of his way, he will keep out of yours.'

It was a strange life, perpetually at hide-and-seek with the priest. When we met in the church—which was rarely, for he preferred to be out of doors with his dogs and falcons—he did not see us. But when we met in the churchyard, face to face among the graves, we would swap civilities and talk in a friendly way of archery and bowls. And on Sundays and feast-days, when the people came to Mass, Gerda and I sat with them, and were duly blessed.

As to our provisioning, that was simple. Abel and Molly arranged it together. Each day one or other would take food to the city gate, where we would collect it, paying from what remained in Corvinus' purse. We had good friends. Even Will Dodd supplied half a boiled fowl one day, saying he liked to be a party to secrets, having so few of his own.

If the Countess knew we still hung about her walls she gave no sign of it, and for a long time we heard nothing either of her or of Lothar.

Apart from the cold, anxiety for Lothar and a general concern for our future, I was quite satisfied to live in the church. Abel got parchment for me, and charcoal, and I began to draw again, first copying the carvings on the choir-stalls, then the screen. I drew Gerda too—Gerda in every attitude, sleeping and waking, walking and still; Gerda crouched in her cloak, shrammed with cold, her pinched face and dishevelled hair; Gerda breaking bread, the round loaf between her square hands; Gerda far away in thought, eyes unfocused. But there was always a shadow on her face. I wanted to draw her smiling and could not, so I tore up all that I had done, which made her weep. Then I drew her weeping, instead.

For her this must have been the sorriest time of all, with so many hours hanging heavy in her hands and no occupation. In the town there had always been the chance of seeing Lothar, however painful that might be. There had been the chance of Lothar seeing her, and perhaps remembering. Here she had nothing. Yet *I* wanted her to smile—and was out of temper because she could not. *I* wanted her to eat hearty and, because she had no appetite, threw the food on the floor in a rage—and then had to gather it up, crumb by crumb, lest the parson see it and be forced to notice us.

Poor Gerda, I was no real friend to her.

Also the church oppressed her. She was afraid of the parson, it was so unnatural that he should never speak, never forget himself enough to smile at her. She would have forgotten a thousand times in a day. Perhaps he *really* did not see her: perhaps she *really* was not there?

'O, Gerda! What *is* real? If you can tell the difference between real and not-real, you are a philosopher and too clever for me.'

I scolded her for foolishness, yet her thoughts were mine. It *was* an unnatural state in which to live; the parson took his part in it unnaturally well. Flitting between the massive pillars, Gerda seemed insubstantial, like a ghost earth-bound by old habit, unable to communicate . . . Perhaps it was the same with me.

'You must take hold of yourself,' I said.

She feared she could not. So she took to wandering in the lanes, returning wet through to the skin, often freezing. She developed a cough which she tried to hide from me—and I was impatient with her, when I should have been gentle. Yet there was no open quarrel—better perhaps if there had been, for quarrels can be mended with love, and fears which are given form lose half their terror. Or so it is said. I loved her and did not know how far we had grown apart.

Ten days or so went by. The church was stripped of its holly and ivy—though whether the wrinkled leaves were burned or buried I never knew—and the crib was taken down. Without the branches and painted figures the place looked very bare, even colder than before.

Gerda was away somewhere, courting her death in the rain. The church was gloomy in the weak light of a winter afternoon and the effigies of the old Count's father and grandfather, though handsomely made, were poor company for a man uncertain of his own existence. I knew how Gerda felt; even the muddy graveyard would be better than this. I went outside to look again at Saint Michael in his niche on the tower.

Already the weather had healed the wound in the stone, where the wing had been lopped off; soon even the scar would fade. The statue no longer looked like something damaged but as though it had been created in this shape. It seemed an omen.

Omens are made to be read, but this was beyond me. I struggled with it, trying various meanings. None fitted well save one—that Lothar had settled here and was satisfied—and this I would not believe. His true beauty and the Lady's falsehood could never match . . .

Then Gerda touched my arm and brought me back to the dull present, which was endurable to me only because I loved her. Loving her, I began at once to blame her for staying so long.

'Matthew,' she said. 'You are going to be very angry with me . . .'

I stopped in mid-accusation. Angry? Impatient, curt, ungentle perhaps—but angry? Never! I smiled to show her how mistaken she was.

'No, Matthew, listen. I don't know how to tell you . . .'

'Then don't tell me,' I said. 'Come inside, wrap yourself up in my cloak and get warm again.' She should not think me angry.

'She was so little, Matthew. Old and shrivelled and small. And she had nothing, Matthew, even less than we. I've a decent cloak and the shelter of this church—though God knows I complain about it. And I'm young still, and have strong hands, and all the years ahead . . .'

She spoke very quickly and very low. I had to strain to hear her.

'She was under the bridge, poor soul, staring at the water. So old and with nothing. So I gave it to her, Matthew. I had to. I thought you wouldn't mind . . . but then I got to thinking . . .

'Oh, say you don't mind . . . I *had* to!'

'Gerda,' I said. 'You gave her what?' And, as God is my witness, I said it patiently.

'All of it,' said Gerda, and began to shake. Her mouth trembled and she tried to still the trembling with her teeth, but her jaw shook and the teeth rattled in her head as though she had an ague. She put up her hands to hide her face—and her hands shook too, and her shoulders jerked. She was afraid of *me*—and it was the saddest and most ugly thing I had ever seen. Even worse, her fear did not move me to pity . . . it made me want to strike her. She saw it in my eyes and made a strong effort to control herself. Poor, brave Gerda. She might as well have tried to quell a storm, or bind the ocean.

I remembered something my old master told me once—that everything in nature is made up of particles, or atoms, of the same stuff, differing only in their arrangement . . . one pattern making stone, another flesh, and so on. A wise man, one Lucretius, had written it all down, he said, in ancient times. I was standing in the great nave of his cathedral when Master Thibaud told me this, and immediately I had felt the whole weight of the building on my shoulders, the tension of each springing arch concentrated at the base of my skull. I heard the stones sing. I was afraid to move, afraid that my clumsiness might disturb the pre-ordained dance of the atoms and set them moving in another path, to bring the entire building down upon my head in a shower of earth—or flowers.

I had forgotten it, together with many other things, until Gerda's violent trembling brought it back to the surface of my mind. I thought, 'My God, she will shake herself into stone!' And I put out my hand, not to strike her, but to hold her still.

'What did you give her?' I said. 'Tell me, Gerda.'

'All our money,' she said. 'Every penny of it, that you had given me to mind.'

What could I say to that?

People who ask, 'What is money, after all?' are usually those who have plenty. The poor know very well what money is. It is bread and bacon-fat and warmth. Gerda knew this as well as I did. Therefore, if she had given away all we had, she must have had good reason.

So I said again, 'Tell me about it, Gerda.' And I swore to her that I was not angry at all.

It was a very little story. She had walked as far as the bridge, she said, because she did not wish to see the city and there were only two ways to go, the third path being mired. Yes, that I understood.

'But when I came to the bridge, the rain was falling . . . and I did not want to come home wet again . . . you were so cross yesterday, because I was wet . . .'

'I'm sorry, Gerda. It is only because I care for you. Just tell me what happened.'

There had been an old woman there, standing under the bridge, almost at the edge of the water. A very old woman, very frail . . .

'And with such terrible shoes, Matthew. Gaping holes in them, and her poor feet bandaged with rags.'

'Yes,' I said. 'It is bad to be a beggar in wintertime, when no one has a crumb to spare and there is no work to be had.'

'I think it must be even worse when one is old,' said Gerda.

She had taken out her purse, our purse, to give the old creature a penny; that was all she meant to do. And then she thought, a penny will buy bread, another penny will buy warm straw to sleep on, another may give her an hour or two by someone's fire.

'That's how it happened, Matthew. A little bit at a time. Then I thought, a silver piece will buy her a new cloak, and this other silver piece means shoes . . . and so it went on till I had counted out every coin and there was nothing left. She was very grateful, Matthew. It was truly a good deed.'

I said nothing. I could not tell her that now we were beggars ourselves, and might well starve before long.

'I only thought afterwards, what I had done. And then I was afraid to come home . . . so I walked about.'

'In the rain, Gerda,' I said, and touched her wet cloak.

'She blessed me,' said Gerda. 'Her blessing warmed me, I'm sure of it. I hardly noticed the rain.'

Well, that was a trifle gained. I hoped the blessing would warm me too.

'And she gave me something in return . . . apart from the blessing. Matthew, don't be angry—and don't laugh. It was all she had.'

She opened her hand and showed me . . . a walnut. I tried to smile.

'It was all she had,' Gerda said, again. 'She said it would bring me my heart's desire, if I used it right. Poor soul, she was crazed with cold.'

'Dear Gerda,' I said. 'You have purchased very little with your purse of money.'

'It was not a purchase,' she insisted. 'I gave her the money and she gave me this. And a rhyme to go with it.'

'A rhyme? O, Gerda! Do you think we are living in a fairy tale? Will a tree grow out of your magic nut, which we have only to climb to find ourselves in a land where banquets are served by invisible hands and the very rivers run wine? Your old woman might have tried her own luck, before you parted with your silver.'

'There,' she said. 'You are angry, after all. And of course you are angry. I don't know what I deserve . . . but, Matthew, it seemed so right at the time. And I thought it might help Lord Lothar.'

She began to cry, holding her hands in front of her face, and I could see the tears falling between her fingers.

'Everything has been so strange, Matthew. This seemed no more strange than anything else . . .'

Yes, Abel had said that people like Lothar let in the night. Admit one and you admit a host of others.

'Well, Gerda, we are penniless,' I said, as gently as I could. 'And we must make the best of it. So tell me the rhyme.'

'At the heart of the maze, where all paths converge,
Unwind the charm and let the truth emerge . . .

'And she said, if my own truth would dare it. That was all, and it doesn't even make sense. But I thought I might understand one day and use it to help Lord Lothar.'

'I have lost track of sense,' I told her. 'Is it a maze we have yet to find, I wonder? Or is the walnut shell a maze? Or is the charm itself a maze we have to penetrate . . .'

It was not important. I had no more faith in Gerda's walnut than I had in Lothar's return—but something good had been bought with our purse. We were at peace together again.

The next morning we took stock of our possessions, such as they were, in the hope of finding something we might sell—and we had more than we thought. There was Gerda's basket which we would not need as we had nothing to put in it, and my knife which was a good blade, very sharp.

'I have nothing to carve,' I said. 'Unless I make a start on the choir-stalls, improving what another man has done. And there's no usefulness in that unless the priest were to pay me, which he won't. When we have eaten my blade and your basket, we will think again. When summer comes, we will eat our cloaks—and who knows what may happen before winter comes round again?'

'Why,' cried Gerda. 'I can always stand under the bridge and sell my walnut for a purse of gold. Then I shall have made a profit for you.'

We met Abel at the city-gate and he took the basket, saying he would get what he could for it but dared not promise much. I no longer worried; we had been hungry before and survived.

Two days after we parted with the basket, Abel came to visit us at the church, bringing with him a small sack of somewhat wrinkled apples which, he claimed, had been given him for the bear's consumption.

'He's sleepy now,' he said. 'He don't want much to eat, and besides, I didn't tell him about the apples so he won't miss them . . .'

'This could have waited till tomorrow,' I said, when I had thanked him. 'You have news for us which you thought would not wait.'

'Not news,' he said. 'Talk only. Rumour.'

Ill rumour I could see, now I looked at him.

The old Count, it was said, had died.

'Who says?'

But there was nothing certain. A stranger at the castle, the Countess shut up with him for half a day, a new spring in her step . . .

'Not enough,' I said. 'A stranger at the castle is hardly news. Why, Abel, Lothar was once a stranger there and closeted with the Countess for longer than half a day if all they say, whoever they be, were true. Perhaps this stranger is plumaged like an eagle or antlered like a stag, and Lothar—who must seem as commonplace now as a pair of old shoes—will—'

'Do you think that, Matthew?'

'No,' I said. 'Do you?'

'The Countess has given him a jewel . . .'

'For God's sake, Abel,' I shouted. 'You sound like a market-woman. Of course the Countess has given him jewels. Do you think

(137)

we are idiots? When last we saw Lothar he was decked with jewels; he was jewelled all over like an emperor's pyx. Did you think he brought so much treasure with him?'

'This is a special jewel,' he said. 'A family jewel. It was the Count's.'

'It signifies nothing,' I said, still too loudly, and not daring to look at Gerda's face. 'Do *they* talk of marriage?'

'Not yet. But, Matthew, it will come. You know it, Gerda knows it. You cannot spare her by pretending it is not likely. So, don't wait for it to happen . . .'

That night, in the dark, Gerda said, 'Matthew, is it true?' And though her voice was scarcely louder than a whisper, the echoes caught it and sent her words round and round until they came back to her. True . . . true . . . true . . .

'Yes,' I said. 'I think it is.'

If silence also can make echoes, hers did. Her silence battered me from every wall. I went to her and held her hands. They were very cold, carved in ice, and mine did nothing to warm them.

I was desperate to comfort her. 'Gerda,' I said. 'There was a goose-girl once, who loved a prince. And he loved her. But a witch-woman made him captive and put a spell on his memory to make him marry her . . .'

'Don't, Matthew, please. I know that story too, and she wasn't a goose-girl, she was a real princess. And she had a magical dress, a wonderful dress which she sold for the right to sleep at the prince's door . . . It's only a story, Matthew. However kindly you mean it, it cannot, cannot help . . .'

She wept. I put my arms round her and she wept in my arms. And then she went to sleep. In the morning she was calm again.

I put the walnut in her hand and closed her fingers over it.

'It was only a story,' I said. 'But stories are often made from bits of truth patched together. Would you have believed in a prince with a swan's wing if you had never seen Lothar?'

'We may have dreamed him,' she said. 'Didn't Abel say so, once? Or something like it?'

'Then the Countess is having a strong dream,' I said. 'If she intends to marry him.'

Gerda opened her fingers very slowly and stared at the walnut. It was as if she were trying to see right through the shell to what might be inside. She looked thin and vulnerable and plain, her face blotched and the fine high cheek-bones too prominent now for any sort of beauty.

'If you love Lothar, you will fight,' I said. 'In the story, the princess had a hazel-nut which she opened to find her magic dress. Try, Gerda, try.'

It was nonsense and I was cruel to make her try, but I could not bear to see her give in and lose her brightness. And during the long wakeful night I had come to believe in the walnut. I thought it shone with a light that came from itself, I thought it responded when I touched it. I thought that it would crack apart and reveal a dress made of moonlight and starlight. I wanted it to be so.

'A purse of silver for your heart's desire. Either we are all mad, Gerda, or it must be true.'

And the nutshell did not break.

Gerda looked at me with pity, just as I looked at her.

'There has to be a maze,' she reminded me. 'It is no use unless we are standing in a maze.'

I have seen mazes in many cathedrals and marvelled at their ingenuity, and at the devotion of those who thread them on their knees, but I have never found one in a more humble church. Nevertheless, I looked. A man who has spent his life in arguing with God is not to be defeated by a walnut and a cryptic rhyme. Wherever there was space enough to set a few tiles together in a pattern, I looked for a maze. I looked behind the altar and in the crypt, in the belfry and in the small low-ceilinged room above the porch where bats slept in the daytime. I crawled about the floor of the nave and counted tiles—so many with griffons on them, and so many with fleurs-de-lys, a score and more with shields, and five with a symbol that was like a wheel. But from whichever side I counted, wherever I began and ended, I could make no pattern of them that was in the least way like a maze.

'Then I will *make* a maze for you,' I said.

'No, Matthew, please.'

'The old woman did not say it had to be a certain sort of maze, did she? Or in a certain place? She did not say go to Chartres, or

Amiens or Poitiers? She did not say it was in Troy Town or in Armorie? Well then, I'll make you a maze and you can stand in that and get your heart's desire.'

The voice I heard did not sound like mine, but I knew it was *my* body that ran into the churchyard, and *my* hands that searched and scrabbled for stones; it was *my* heart that banged against my ribs and *my* lungs that laboured with my breath. Yet it seemed to me I stood outside and watched, quite apart from what was happening. And I said, into the head of the wild man who was tearing down a corner of the churchyard wall: 'No, Matthew. It cannot be done as you are doing it. You cannot impose a maze where no maze is.'

Then Gerda ran out of the church and shouted, 'Leave it, Matthew.'

But I—or he, the man who was using my body—would not leave it. Already he had a sizeable heap of stones at his side and the hole in the wall was big enough to pass a coffin through. Gerda dragged at his arm but he flung her away and went back to the work, his fingers bleeding. Gerda stood at the church door, her mouth wide open in her white face, and screamed, 'Leave it. Leave it. Leave it,' as though she would never stop.

And the voice that was not quite mine was yelling too.

Then Lothar and the Lady came riding by, on the road from the city. If they saw the tumbled wall or heard the noise we made, they did not show it. I think they were so wrapped about in their own snow-silence they noticed nothing at all that was outside themselves. Lothar's wing was spread behind the Countess so that she was seen, as it were, against a falling curtain of feathers and the only colour between the two of them was the jewel that Lothar wore on his breast, a great red stone that drew light into itself and kept it there.

Their beauty, their whiteness and their silence brought me back into myself. I was Matthew, sucking my raw knuckles by a rough pyramid of stones, and feeling pain where the driving rage had been. Gerda said, 'Leave it, Matthew,' in her own quiet voice, choked, and went into the church again.

They rode on up the hill, and for a long time I stood, listening to the music of their harness bells, and feeling spent. What use to make a maze? It could make no difference now. There was no magic in all the world that was stronger than the Lady's and Gerda's heart's desire must remain where it was hid, inside a walnut shell that would not be cracked.

Well, whatever happened or did not happen, I must mend the wall. I collected together all the stones I had scattered about among the graves, and began to build again. Some were pieces of rock so large I marvelled at my own strength in moving them—and at my madness in thinking I could use them in a maze. And, because I was myself again, I began to be aware of the texture of the stones, to wonder at their grain and the way it governed their shapes. These were not fine stones but serviceable, stones chosen for building because they would stand for ever. They were as old as God. Some were whorled like shells and some had ferns in them and one, the largest of all, had something impressed in it that looked like the bones of a wing. This I hid behind other smaller stones for I did not want Gerda to see it for fear it should make her even more unhappy.

When I had finished building the wall, I looked round for something else to do. If my hands were occupied I would not have to think; I would not have to remember that I had frightened Gerda or wonder how to set things right.

But there was nothing that needed to be done, nothing that I could see. Then I thought of Saint Michael, who had grown accustomed to his single wing, and I made myself see him once more as damaged, an object to be mended.

'Old Woman's magic,' I told myself. 'Mend Saint Michael and I'll mend Lothar!'

First I must see if it were possible to get the statue down without a pulley and tackle; if not, I would have to improvise—my cloak for a cradle, Abel could get me a rope and, with luck, there might be a staple already in the wall.

I began to climb the tower, and found it easier than I had guessed. The carvings on the porch helped me, and then there was a lancet window, then a ledge. From there I could reach, with the tips of my fingers, the lowest coil of the serpent on which Saint

Michael stood—and there I stopped. Before attempting the next stage of my climb, I would have to plan it. To go straight up, clinging with fingernails and toes to the rough wall, was one way but, I thought, not the best. Crouched eye to eye with the statue, I would be too close. Better to get above the niche and come down again a little to the side. I moved along the ledge toward the great stepped buttress that supported the tower. In its angle I would be able to rest, secure from the wind, while I decided what to do . . .

From here I could see the whole world. There was the road we had travelled in the autumn, coming to this place, and there the path we had left. If only we had avoided the road, crossed over it, to continue in our original direction . . . I edged round the buttress to see where that path led and, with my eyes, followed its windings over a dozen hills before I lost it.

Beyond the hills lay marshy country, only partly drained. The straight lines that struck across it must be ditches and, somewhere among them, the path would go on—it could not simply stop. There were some low hills with houses on them, and fields that had been reclaimed, and I supposed the path must link them together, like beads on a rosary, though I could not see it. Almost idly I traced a meander between each group but somehow it failed to work. The ditches created barriers. I followed the ditches and then the hills were in the way. It was like a maze.

I leaned out from the buttress and shouted, 'GERDA!'

Brave Gerda! It was not so long since she had been in terror of my madness—now she came running because I called her name.

When she saw me leaning out from my perch like a misplaced gargoyle, I think all her fear returned—she put her hand over her mouth and her eyes went wild.

'I want to show you something,' I called down to her.

And she laughed, not laughter to humour a madman, but real laughter.

'Matthew,' she called back. 'I cannot climb a tower in skirts. You must come down instead, and tell me about it.'

'Not the outside, Gerda, the inside. The tower has stairs, climb them, woman, and make haste.'

While she climbed up within, I climbed down without, and

followed her up the twisting stairs to the parapet above the bell-chamber.

'Now, Gerda,' I said. 'What do you see?'

If there *were* a maze in the marsh and I had not imagined it, she would see it for herself—but if I told her what to look for, she would see that, to please me. It is one of the more irritating ways of women.

So, a little puzzled, Gerda looked.

'Hills, a few houses . . . are they houses, Matthew? Paths and ditches—'

'Did you say paths?'

'Why, yes. There are four, I think . . . no. Five. And all meeting in one place, if one could only get there. But look, there's a clump of trees in the way of this, and a ditch to be leapt there. And this one stops one side of a hill and starts again at the other. If you want to reach the centre, you have to keep going back and beginning again—'

She saw more than I did.

'I saw no paths,' I said. 'Only ditches. Could you get to the centre, do you think?'

'Not easily. But, Matthew, it's a maze, isn't it? Is that what I had to see?'

Then the old familiar shadow marred her face.

'But it's no use, is it, without him?'

'I don't know. The charm might work from a distance, but I don't know. Did your old woman say nothing else?'

Nothing that Gerda could remember.

'We'll try it,' I said. 'With or without Lothar. We'll go to-morrow.'

But tomorrow brought sleet and ice.

Rain, sleet, ice and a bitter wind—thus the weather held for days. Only once the sun rose on what promised to be a brighter morning, and within an hour the rain set in again.

Yet—snow, hail or driving sleet—Abel was constant, bringing us the scraps of food he said his bear rejected, and the town's gossip for salt. The old Count's death was now made public, he told us, but this we knew already, having heard it from the pulpit and said our prayers for his soul's rest. The Countess, he added, had worn mourning for a day. And yes, there was a little talk of marriage but it was speculative, merely. Some said one thing and some another, and no one knew which to take for gospel. But a woman on an outlying farm had given birth to a litter of rabbits—and that was a portent of evil, alarming enough to pack all the churches with anxious sinners—whether it were true or not. The Countess herself had ridden over to see the woman and come back in a towering rage, saying it was all fraud. Even so, it was not an auspicious time to be thinking of weddings.

I asked what he knew of the marsh country beyond the hills, but he had never been there.

'I like my land to be land and my water, water,' he said. 'Though I'd stretch a point if there was money to be gained—which there's not. Marsh folk spend all they get in keeping the wet back. But it still seeps in, regardless. Why?'

'That's where we're going,' I said, carelessly. 'When the sky clears.'

'I wouldn't. You'll lose yourselves, or stray onto the wrong paths and drown, trying to find your way out again.'

'Are there so many paths?'

'Only one right one, the causeway. The others are treacherous, they come and go. It's said there were five once, all leading to the centre, but they've been lost since . . .'

'How lost?'

He shrugged, 'Drowned, maybe. They appear and disappear, like ghosts of paths. Some see them, others don't.'

If there were paths as unreliable as this, I said, we would need to know of them.

'Look,' Abel said. 'We started on the wrong foot, when we met. I tried to make money out of you, matching your freakish friend with the Lady, when I should have warned you instead. I gave him the tip that sent him off; I feel responsible, d'ye see?'

It was very dark in the church but I could see he sweated, even in the cold.

'We met again when you came to save my bear from hurt and, for that alone, I'd want to make amends for the first. So I'm warning you now. Just don't go there. Good advice is better than any map, Matthew, so listen. No marsh was ever friendly to folk not bred on it. Marsh folk keep to themselves and marry their cousins; the water hides what secrets they have. And they don't like strangers.'

'There's more than this,' I said. 'Moorland folk don't like strangers either, and neither do mining folk. The country doesn't like the town and the town works hard to keep the country out. That's not enough to make you sweat.'

I wanted to know more about the centre. If five paths once met there, it must have been a place of some importance. But Abel knew nothing definite. The centre, like the paths, had drowned—and no one went there. Not if they wanted to come back.

I said, 'Wherever there's water, there's a story of a drowned city.' But Abel said it was not a city. Neither, as far as he knew, was it a church.

'What then?'

'An atmosphere. A state of mind. A place of dreams. But whatever it was once don't signify. The water's above it now. Take my advice and try another road.'

When he saw that we were determined to go, no matter what he said, he pressed some coins into my hand, muttering that it was in payment for something I had done for him once and forgotten— Abel could never make a gift outright . . .

'It's a long road,' he said. 'And you'll need food—for the first stretch anyway. Keep out of the wood. And when you get to the place where the track begins to go downhill—come back.'

He would not say goodbye, but gave me a piece of iron to carry in my pouch, not that he thought it much protection where we were going, but better than nothing at all. And he looked back, twice, to wave.

I could not decide whether he knew a great deal more about the marsh than he had told us, or much less, and while I was debating it in my mind, trying to disentangle facts from hints, I began to wonder why we were going there at all—to relieve Lothar of his wing? To give Gerda her heart's desire? The rhyme spoke only of truth.

'Gerda,' I said. 'What *is* your heart's desire?' But she must have been asleep, for she did not answer.

The sun had set amid red clouds and the next day was fine. Gerda was ready to start at once, but I said we should make a map first. If the paths were as uncertain as Abel said, it would be as well to know in advance where they began and ended. And, try as I might, I was still unable to distinguish their windings among the hills and ditches.

So, in charcoal, on one of my torn parchments, Gerda made a map—a very simple one, with the ditches marked in wavy lines for water, and with circles for hills, one with a cross on it for the building I took to be a church, and with little squares to mark the houses.

'It will do,' I said, but doubtfully. 'Are you sure about the paths?'

She was quite sure. She said there was no danger of our getting lost.

And now it was our last night in the church. I spent one of Abel's coins on ceremony and lit two candles to the Mother of God, to bless our journey. It was what Gerda called thrifty extravagance; having made the offering, we shared the light.

I wondered if the priest would miss us. That very morning he had stood for more than half an hour, turning the pages of his breviary while I read it over his shoulder. I was so close to him, my breath must have warmed his neck, and he had not even rolled an eye in my direction. Being in the church, I was invisible. An hour later, at the lych gate, he told me his best dog had colic and he was at his wits' end what to do. I wished I could have thanked him for his hospitality. He had done his best for us, according to his lights, and offended no one.

And we should have taken leave of Lothar. What we were about to do concerned him very closely. Whatever might happen when Gerda brought the walnut to the centre of the maze, it would change something for Lothar. Supposing it were on his wedding-day that he exchanged his feathers for an arm, how would the Lady take it? Yet the rhyme was not specific. *Unwind the charm*, it said— but Lothar was under a double enchantment—would he simply wake from his Lady's snow-sleep and remember Gerda's greater worth? Then he would have to follow her and the whole tale would begin again, the quest for another walnut and another maze.

'What?' said Gerda, breaking in on my thoughts. 'Did you speak?'

'No. Unless I thought aloud . . .'

'Someone spoke,' she said, uneasily, and looked over her shoulder. But the church was dark save for the candles at the Virgin's feet, and they lit the wall behind her, and ourselves, but little else.

'Yes. I spoke . . .'

And Lothar came toward us out of the dark of the nave into our small light, Lothar in his old shabby tunic and the cloak Gerda had patched for him with cloth torn from her shift.

'They shot Barney,' he said, and knelt down at Gerda's feet, holding out to her the bundle he carried cradled in his wing.

She took it from him and began very slowly to undo the cloths that wrapped her gander's carcass. Lothar had shrouded him richly in grey velvet lined with miniver, rose-coloured silk and fine white linen. Poor Barney, he had never bedded so softly in all his life. Gerda stroked the breast of her dead bird, her fingers first avoiding and then gently touching the stained feathers near the wound.

'Dear Barney,' she said. 'He was all talk and bombast, he never hurt a soul.'

'So why, Lothar, why?' I demanded. 'There's not even sport to be had in shooting a tame gander.'

'He was a jest at first. He followed me about as though he were my twin—or my conscience. I had forgotten all of you, but he made it his duty to remind me. And, Gerda, there were times when I almost remembered—but the waking of my memory brought so much pain with it, I was glad to resist and let it sleep again.'

'He left one of your feathers in the church,' I said. 'He did what he could.'

'He was always there,' said Lothar, flinching. 'So they grew tired of him. And when they were tired of him, they killed him. As they would have done with me, I think, sooner or later. Though perhaps not with arrows . . .'

I nodded. 'The old Count died in prison when a little money would have bought him out. But you were a caged bird anyway, Lothar, *you* would have needed to learn new tricks to keep alive.'

Gerda wrapped the bird again and laid it aside.

'Tell us everything,' she said. 'And then it will be over for you.'

'I can tell you,' he said, his hand reaching for Gerda's. 'But much of it you would never understand'. You are too simple, Gerda. In your world the sun rises and sets, willy-nilly, every day; men work with their hands and most folk are good—even though you might have to dig deep to find their goodness. Almira's world is not like that. The sun rises only because she wills it, and sets only when she is weary. Everything is a game to be abandoned as soon as it begins to stale. Goodness is for mocking. How could *you* ever understand that world?'

'How could *you* ever live in it?' she countered.

'I thought it suited me,' he said. I was glad his face was turned so that I could not see it, his voice held so much bitterness. 'Because I am a freak of nature, I thought I might be happy in a place where nature was shut out. And I was drawn to Almira's world from the moment I saw her. In one way, Gerda, it *was* the right place for me. The Lady had a special liking for . . . freaks. I did not have to hide from anyone.'

I looked at Gerda. Hunger and privation had pared her to the bone, but her mouth was very sweet still, when she smiled. And I thought of the Lady, lying so white and burning among Lothar's feathers, with her white hair and silver eyes.

'Barney saved you,' I said, harshly. 'He meant to do it somehow, and he did. It was because he died that you remembered. His death wasn't wasted.'

'It might have been,' said Lothar, shivering. 'A little longer and it might have been.'

I went away, by myself, into the dark body of the church and stood with my face pressed against a pillar, my back to the rood. I was very angry. I said, God, you did not have to kill a valiant bird to show me what the cross means. If you are all-knowing and all-powerful, you could have found some other way.

I waited a long while for God to answer, but he did not, so I went back to Gerda and Lothar and poor dead Barney.

The candles flared brightly and then, one after the other, died. In total darkness we were more at ease together; our old friendship reasserted itself and we were able to forget the hurt our eyes still registered while there was light to see. Our bodies moved closer for warmth. As I dropped into sleep, Lothar stirred and his feathers brushed my face.

We buried Barney, in his linen and fine silk, his grey velvet and miniver, at the place where the roads crossed at the top of the hill, and we heaped a cairn of stones above his grave, to mark it. His loyalty deserved a better memorial, we all knew, but we had neither the means nor the time to see to it. At least the sun shone on his burying, later we thought it would never shine again.

By afternoon the sky was swollen with black clouds and, from then on, it rained steadily, hour after hour, day after day. Every stream became a river and every river a raging torrent. We lost our path quite soon and wandered a long time without direction, the whole landscape obscured by rain. Gerda's cough worsened; she walked with one hand tight against her side, protesting that we were not to worry, it was already much easier—and then coughed again so violently she was almost torn apart.

I remember very little of our journey—except for the rain. We slept one night in a stone hut, shaped like a beehive, and were very cramped there, so that we could scarcely stand when we crawled out next morning.

And another night we spent in a wood where trailing wisps of fog hung from the branches and moved, as though they were alive, from tree to tree. It was a most unnatural fog and clung to us in a curiously tenacious way. I have never, before or since, known fog that could be brushed away like cobweb. And, in brushing it away, I was almost overpowered by an intense and unassuageable sadness; I felt as I would have done in rejecting a hungry, and perhaps wounded, animal. It was a feeling from which I could not rid myself during all the time we stayed in the wood, and it even seemed to me that we should remain there, rather than cause the fog more grief. Both Lothar and Gerda felt it too, for Gerda was weeping quietly as she walked and Lothar, when we were once more in the open, turned back to hang a stray wisp over a twig. Then he seemed reluctant to go on and continued to look behind him until the wood was out of sight. We none of us spoke of it.

I do not know where or when we lost Gerda's precious map, or how many days went by before we reached the marsh. But I remember a farmhouse built of mud and wooden beams, where we begged for food and were driven away by a fierce woman who pelted us with turnips, and screamed, 'Beggars! Vagabonds! Thieves! Murderers!' with her hair escaping from her cap and tumbling down over her neck—but whether that were at the beginning or near the end of our journey I cannot say. I know we were grateful for the turnips.

And I remember a bridge made of flat pieces of stone, very low above the water, and a slanting field that had armour in it—an ancient helmet and part of a breastplate, rusting in the rain.

And a cave with the cold ashes of a fire at its mouth. It was here I found the statue of a woman, small enough to hold in the palm of one hand, and very ugly, with a knob for a head and her legs broken off at the knees. From certain cuts, deeply scored, I judged her to be the great-grandmother of the witch-i'-the-wall and left her where she was, at the back of the cave among pieces of broken pot, for someone else to find.

These things I remember clearly as separate pictures, very small and sharp—but I do not know in what order they belong, and I do not know how time arranged itself. We may have rested as often as we walked.

There were many other things, less clear—a Christ crucified on an oak tree, alone in a wide empty space; a cowled priest sitting at a chess board on which the pieces moved by their own will; a swirling pool with faces in it, all the faces I have ever seen.

Lothar and Gerda may have seen other images, not these. Lothar smiled sometimes, secretly, yet I think he would not have smiled at the things I saw. And once Gerda cried, 'Look!' and began to run toward something neither of us could see.

And all the time, it rained.

At some point, our way—if one can call such meandering a way—must have taken a downward turn, but so gradually that we did not notice it until we found ourselves on the slope of a hill with sky on three sides of us and the grey-green marsh below. We stood and gazed.

'Five paths,' said Gerda.

But I saw only the rows of pollarded willows, a few low islands with houses on them, the squat tower of a church and a wide expanse of water.

I said, 'Are you sure, Gerda?'

'Quite sure.'

'Lothar?'

'Yes,' he said. 'Five paths.'

We went down, slowly on the slippery grass; the rain turned to a cold white mist which lifted momentarily to show a causeway leading into emptiness.

Gerda said, 'The paths will be easier to follow now that the ditches have broken their banks.'

And I saw that the causeway was broken too. It would not take us far toward the centre—wherever that might be.

Then we were on the causeway. Gerda hesitated, peering about her.

'I think it must be this one,' she said, and stepped into the mist. I followed, expecting to be swept away and drowned, but there *was* a path under my feet, just below the surface of the water. And, though I could not see it, it was firm.

I saw Lothar bend his head to Gerda's. Perhaps he kissed her, I was not near enough to see, but she put up her hands as though she would cling to him, then dropped them again. It was a small gesture, very humble, and very moving. Epics, in the grand sweep of their telling, ignore such things—but surely every hero is given a little push on his way by a woman standing behind him, a woman like Gerda who is not sure what she does but accepts her place in the pattern. The landscape was desolate—grey marsh and grey sky—but it was not more desolate than Gerda.

Now it was Lothar who went ahead. Sometimes we saw him plainly and sometimes the mist enveloped him so entirely that we could follow only the sound his feet made, splashing through the still rising water . . .

I caught hold of Gerda's shoulders and spun her round to face me. Her eyes were huge and dark, the iris covering all the blue so that they were not like Gerda's eyes at all.

'Gerda,' I said. 'Do you know what you are doing?'

She knew. And her heart's desire was that Lothar should be

whole again, as he was meant to be—not that he should love her. She was too proud to use magic for that.

'Are you certain it is what you want?'

'I am quite certain.'

'If this works,' I said, 'if there is any truth in it, you may lose everything. Have you thought of that?'

I could not bring myself to say, 'You may lose Lothar.' God knows she had lost everything else.

'I have thought of it,' she said. 'Often.'

'A prince with a swan's wing is exceptional,' I said. 'He is outside of time, outside reality. He can walk the whole world with a goose-girl for company, and for most of the world it is nothing more than a passing marvel—a fireside story told to entertain. For most of the world. But, for you, Gerda, it can last as long as you like—if you choose . . .'

'I have thought of it,' she said, again.

'Have you? Have you thought of everything? You will be giving Lothar the life that was his before the enchantment bound him. His sister is a duchess, his brothers are princes, his life in that world will be different from anything you have known. And there may well be no place in it for a goose-girl—though she were ten times as beautiful as you, and ten times as good. You may lose him altogether, Gerda.'

'I know,' she said. 'But I faced that already, back there.'

Then she said, 'We are almost at the centre of the maze.'

I let her go and we went on again, still following Lothar.

Suddenly the mist cleared and I saw the path, just as Gerda saw it, one of five winding through the marsh, and the causeway behind us, and the spreading lake that covered the fields and crept toward the distant homesteads. Beyond the houses, where the land was higher, stood the church with its strong, square tower. And the bells were ringing to call the people in, to keep them safe until the flood receded.

Lothar waited for us to come up with him. He stood on a hummock of coarse grass and I saw that there all the paths met and ended. Perhaps time ended and began there too—such places must exist.

'Now!' said Gerda, and she cracked the nut. Between her hands

(153)

the two halves of the shell separated and fell away. And it was empty. Had I ever expected more?

Had I really expected some instantaneous miracle, a happy ending rolled small as a skein of silk? I had listened to too many tales in which the kitchen-maid exchanged her rags for a gown woven of the sun and moon and danced with a prince for three nights in a row. In life it is quite otherwise. The dead mother's bones might cry for ever under the juniper tree, I thought, and no one would hear them. In life the nutshell drops empty from the goose-girl's hand, and the rain falls without end.

So it seemed as we stood, the three of us, at the centre of a dissolving world. The two halves of the shell floated away and nothing had changed. Lothar still wore his beautiful, despised wing.

So at what precise moment did the unwinding of the spell begin? With the cracking of the nut—but so subtly that it seemed to me, and to Gerda, that nothing at all had happened? Or was there indeed the pause I now think I remember, a pause as though time held its breath, as though the particles in nature halted in their dance?

The rain still fell. It blurred all edges and made one element of marsh and sky—and it separated Lothar from us.

Then we saw him change.

We saw his nature join with the landscape that was his and not ours, water and air mixed. For the length of a heart-beat he became all swan and then man again, bewildered, flexing the muscles of an arm long unused. But the swan's blood still coursed in his veins, and the pattern shifted and shifted again behind the mist . . . and he was, at once, a man with a swan's head, a swan with a man's face, a winged man, a cloaked swan . . . a creature born of two opposed worlds, who could live in neither.

I would have closed Gerda's eyes if I had dared—but she had left her simple life for this, the unbinding of Lothar. However terrible, it was a part of her choice . . . and I was outside. I put my arms round her and held her close.

And still they struggled together, man and swan, now one and now the other overcoming. I wonder if Lothar suffered at all, or if his feeling soul were able to stand aside, watching as we watched, while nature, undecided, ran wild through his body.

'Unwind the charm and let the truth emerge.' So the old woman had said—and added, 'If your own truth will dare it.'

Gerda's truth was both brave and clear. There was neither self nor selflessness in it and it would dare anything. It had dared to face the unbinding of her love—though it should leave her utterly bereft—and when the affronted air ceased at last to shudder about Lothar and we saw that he was indeed and unmistakably a swan, from his sleek head to his wide webbed feet, it could dare to face that too. Though I think it broke her heart.

The swan, that had so lately been Lothar, stretched his neck to the grey sky and spread both wings, beating back the rain, then stooped and with his golden beak fastidiously stroked a disarranged breast feather into place. He was beautiful still. He stepped into the water, floated a while, pleased with his reflection, then raised himself, treading the surface with faster and faster strides, spray in a bright wake behind, and his wings making the first movements of flight. The air took his weight, he swooped above us, circled once—and flew away.

That was the end of Lothar's story.

And it might well have been the end of ours. When the water had risen above our knees and I was quite sure we must drown before long, we were rescued by a man in a flat-bottomed boat and taken to the church which rode, like a second ark, above the flood. Abel had been quite wrong about the marsh folk—they were good to us, though we could pay nothing and God knew they had little enough for themselves, with all their substance spoiled by the water and most of their livestock dead.

The flood receded. I helped to dig new ditches and to make the banks good, as far as that was possible with only mud for building and no stone to make them strong. Then it was time for me to leave.

Gerda stayed behind with the marsh folk. She had been very ill and would not be strong enough to undertake a journey. Not yet. Perhaps not ever. But I must not worry, they said. They would take good care of her.

'Poor maid,' they said. 'Her soul's gone away with the swans.' Which meant, on the marsh, that she had lost the will to live. I could not have left her in better care.

Before I went away I asked them about the centre of the marsh, the place where the paths met, but they did not like to speak of it. It was an old place, they said, which puzzled me, and when I asked further they said that their grandfathers took it to be the place where God stood when he made the world.

'And then he covered it with water, to make sure no man should stand there after him and make what he had no right to make . . .'

As for me, I came here, found work and settled down—it has been a long road from the woods where I played with the wild cat's kittens and carved her image.

Now there is a Christ of my carving lying under sacks in a side-chapel and soon I will see it raised to its place above the altar. I am quite sure it is the finest thing my hands have yet shaped— but it is not perfect. This Christ will never step down from his cross and walk, nor stoop from it to lift the world in his arms toward the salvation the church promises—nor will any other Christ of mine—and it no longer troubles me. I do not think it will trouble me again.

All the same, I have not become humble in my age. My thumb-print is everywhere in this house of God, so that wherever I turn in it I see my mark, even in the chapter-house where I have set a portrait of myself peering from behind the Archdeacon's chair, cocking a derisive eyebrow at the church's dignitaries for as long as the building will stand. And opposite me, Gerda's face looks out in anguished disapproval. Gerda is everywhere, in all moods, and always with geese near.

But not Lothar. I have never carved Lothar—nor ever will. Perhaps I am a little afraid that, in doing so, I might bind him again within the form he hated. Neither have I ever carved a swan.